THE DREAMER IN THE DREAM

The creative union of artist and author, Jane Adams, and philosopher, Alan Jacobs, has produced an exquisite collection of short stories that are quite simply spellbinding. Examining profound truths through the art of charming and beguiling story-telling, they have composed a beautiful and utterly unique compendium of eccentric tales that may be enjoyed by both children and adults alike. A sheer delight!

Paula Marvelly, author of *Women of Wisdom, Teachers of the One*

O-Books, the publishers of *The Dreamer in the Dream*, set out to produce works that challenge the academic and public norm. This text evokes that strange Alice in Wonderland world that many people live in, in their day and night dreams, except here the implication is that it is not one of fantasy, but the frontier between external and internal reality, which gives access to what is really true to the Self.

Zev ben Shimon Halevi, Kabbalah Society

The Dreamer in the Dream

A Collection of Tales

developed from some ideas
and first drafts by Alan Jacobs
& his Children

The Dreamer in the Dream

A Collection of Tales

developed from some ideas
and first drafts by Alan Jacobs
& his Children

Jane Adams

BOOKS

Winchester, UK
Washington, USA

First published by O-Books, 2012
O-Books is an imprint of John Hunt Publishing Ltd., Laurel House, Station Approach,
Alresford, Hants, SO24 9JH, UK
office1@jhpbooks.net
www.johnhuntpublishing.com

For distributor details and how to order please visit the 'Ordering' section on our website.

Text copyright: Jane Adams 2010

ISBN: 978 1 84694 982 1

A CIP catalogue record for this book is available from the British Library.

Design: Lee Nash

Printed in the USA by Edwards Brothers Malloy

We operate a distinctive and ethical publishing philosophy in all
areas of our business, from our global network of authors to
production and worldwide distribution.

CONTENTS

Preface

The ideas for this collection of esoteric short stories were first jotted down in the early 1990s. This gives them an old fashioned, timeless and rather tongue in cheek flavour, similar to a children's story book.

On finding their raw material in one of Alan Jacobs' notebooks, I felt inspired to work on them myself, which he ageed to. In due course, a couple of tales by Alan's children Graham Jacobs and Dr Laura Jacobs (which he had told them when they were small) were added to the collection, giving it a "family flavour". The collaboration includes many spiritual influences, particularly from Gurdjieff-Ouspensky, the late Douglas Harding, J.Krishnamurti and a blend of wisdom from the esoteric east and west. Alan's love of poetry is highlighted in *Perceval Marlowe goes to a Poetry Class*. The idea here, is that the creative principles which inspire our life and all interior work, come to life in the vessels of ancient harmony with nature. The progressive force from within the roots, is a living paradox. In *The Kettle*, a political situation recurs, whose cast has become archetypal. The tales sometimes work as an oracle. The central story, the *Dreamer within the Dream*, is an essay on death, the after-life and rebirth. It is based on Ouspensky's theme of recurrence, but contains food for thought in any dimension.

The rather baroque style in parts, is deliberate. As we are all young at heart, in approaching the Greater Mysteries, situations of innocence collide with worldly old saws. Each tale explores in different situations, often humorous, a paradoxical edge where the inner and outer life is about to transform.

An imaginative short story may sometimes crack open a hidden kernel which study and meditation cannot by themselves, quite reach.

The book is illustrated by some of my esoteric drawings, including those influenced by the late Douglas Harding - see *Space for the World to Happen in*, p.67.

Jane Adams
February 2011, London

Biographical Notes

JANE ADAMS, born in 1949, is a student of the Tree of Life, Alchemy and Astrology in the western esoteric tradition. She integrated this with her studies in Indian Advaita. Jane began drawing, painting, and writing stories from a very early age. These are her creative tools for the spiritual quest. For many years she was a portrait painter, her commissions include one of Princess Alice of Gloucester, which hangs in the Royal Academy of Music. Jane is now at work on a gallery of portraits of friends and benefactors of the charity Human Rights Aid, as well as preparing collections of her poetry for publication. Additionally, *The Sacred India Tarot* by Rohit Arya and Jane Adams, is due for publication in 2011, by Group Impressions in Mumbai. This other project, bridging eastern and western esotericism, includes her 78 paintings of the Tarot Arcana, powerfully expressed through Indian spiritual archetypes. Jane lives in West Hampstead, London, near her daughter Marisa.

ALAN JACOBS, born in 1929, has made a lifelong study of mysticism, and is Chairman of the Ramana Maharshi Foundation UK. He is a regularly published author and poet, and an accomplished anthologist. He compiled the highly acclaimed *Poetry of the Spirit*, and assembled and edited *The Essential Gnostic Gospels*, *Native American Wisdom, Tales from Rumi*, and the beautiful poetic translation of *The Upanishads* in the 'Sacred Texts' series.

Jane and Alan were married for ten years, during which the first of Alan's anthologies, *Poetry of the Spirit*, was published. They continue as friends, to inspire and help each other creatively. The collection includes two "cautionary tales" by Alan's children Graham and Laura from his first marriage. GRAHAM JACOBS is a senior partner at St James Place partnership Wealth

Management. Dr LAURA JACOBS Bsc. M.A., PhD., specializes in John Milton studies.

The Book of Bennett

ADRIAN BENNETT had an appointment with his tailor. During his morning shave he reflected, as was often his wont, upon the character of this long and interesting lifetime which he was so deeply enjoying, and upon the existence of "he" who appears (in the mirror) to be the principal actor.

Who is Adrian?

> *"His charm and rich anecdotal conversation endear him to all his friends, for his long career in the Diplomatic Service took him to all parts of the globe. The many difficult challenges and tests which he has met - too numerous to recount, for the memories of a man of seventy would fill too many volumes - have exhilarated him. Sometimes when in ironic mode, he coins to himself the phrase: 'this task of Shakespeare no jacket holds'."*

What indeed, off-the-peg, bespoke or hardback deluxe, could cover the untold verse within each volume?

At this point, Adrian smiled at his reflection as he grimaced to scrape an oblong of pine-scented soap from his upper lip (he had old-fashioned habits). He would, as always, shrug his shoulders gracefully into the fitting as given; he admitted with the humility born of many errors, that no title or endpaper can "suit" so great a Work.

> *"As in the life of everyman,"* (so continued the narrative process of Adrian Bennett as was customary during his waking hours) *"he contains within the appearance of himself, a novel much stranger than fiction. There have been relationships intimate, professional, and broken. There have been humour and blame, and*

the making and losing of money. He has built his house in many homes, and repeatedly witnessed birth and bereavement in the great drama of family life - re-negotiating currency in sex, marriage and power. He and those who know him, played the field. They, like young stallions, were turned out to grass to sniff the wind and detect that delectable mare 'the intuitive hunch' in international tensions. They have known worldly success, public acclamation and utter failure. The overall balance of Bennett's Knighthood, hovering between red and black, is emerging generally as 'earthy grey'."

Yes, the same old fascinating story. What of it all?

Adrian dipped his razor into the basin, shook it vigorously in the veiled water and let it sink, as he removed his eyes from his reflection. He began again to think about the very secret book which lies locked in a box inside his Safe. This, for 'Now', was far more interesting. Over many long years he has been writing it, really writing it, but who has ever seen it? The awakening of the book is warm within him. Leaving his face half finished, he turned, paced along the dim corridor, entered his library and turned on the light - for it was still dark - to investigate. The library in the heart of his house is his inner sanctum.

* * *

There, later that same day, we find him again. A warm bright fire in the grate is well established, fed from a basket of apple wood he chopped himself. Upon white ash in the cleansing spirit of fire, are interwoven myriad patterns of incarnation. So a watcher may gaze into the embers and see, in fragile castles of carbon before it falls to ash, whole histories. Poised in translation, immobile, are chunks of dark wood warmed right through and about to fly.

A dreamer is a traveller right on the spot, with his or her ear to the ground. The box in the wall behind one of the tall bookcases stood open; the pages of Adrian's manuscript lay scattered over the hearth-rug near the fire, and Adrian himself on his knees crouched, was reading them.

The hall-mark of the inner aristocrat is borne by one who knows that no garment designed by man can truly attire him. And so he consents to shrug lean shoulders gracefully into the 'fit' provided. Here lies the secret of his attitude to grace: detachment. Carrying the cross of his appearances with elegance and discrimination, such a man wears the intimate contour of his body as he wears his clothes, his house and coat of arms, with a delicate casualness, like an old slipper. His tailor measures and cuts to allow for 'give' to all seasons, and the chosen fabric tends towards well-worn natural hues of earth, stone, sea and a touch of aubretia. The wearer effortlessly emanates 'style' in the faded and untidy grandeur of his home, his gongs, disappointments and accoutrements. Those who behold him, and think his fragrance stems from wealth and landed privilege, do not know it is the fruit of his suffering. The innate quality of spiritual aristocracy, a passionate inward dispassion, bears title to the chequered deeds of many a bandit, and many a birth.

Such is the double life of Adrian Bennett GCMG, of the Most Distinguished Order of St Michael and St George. None know of the book within him, that has no covers. To society he offers the smooth shaven cheek of wit and worldly affairs, and to his own self - wincing at the deceptions from which he has learned, and continues to learn - a deep study of his own life and that of others: the art of contemplation. For longer than he can remember, he was committed to his silent faculty to observe. As a child he spoke little, but learned to play ball and to use his fists accurately with his peers; his public schooling knocked parts of him 'into shape'. Unlike most however, he never lost his curiosity. He learned by painful force of circumstance, to keep the diamond concealed. What was he really alive for? He would say to himself - to 'crack the nut' of humanity, his own. And so for him the noble motto of his Order: AUSPICIUM MELIORIS AEVI - Token of a better age - has never been a mere decoration.

Adrian's library reflects his double tendency. On the left of the room as you go in, the shelves carry handsome editions of the world's fiction old and new - at one, time he was a collector - a vintage Encyclopaedia Britannica, a thoughtful conference of philosophy, logic and psychology, and some beautifully illus-trated gazetteers, maps and accounts of travel and exploration. Here also reside thought-provoking dramatists, poets and anthologies of art and architecture.

But to the right of the room a motley collection is found. Political history and debate rub shoulders with Philo of Alexandria and Greek mythology ... quantum physics and astronomy with Plotinus and other sages ancient and modern ... yoga manuals with Kepler's *Harmonice Mundi*; and books on gardening, with Buddhism. Here also, many curious esoteric volumes, mostly hidden in unidentifiable patterned covers, nestle arcanely with the battered works of Dante, Spenser, Tennyson, Shelley, Browning, and some obscure Romantics. When these crowded shelves are drawn a little out into the room on castors, they give access to Bennet's Safe where the manuscript is stored. The shelf which normally conceals it, betrays an unexpected interest in Russian music, and in dervish forms of Islamic dance.

Most who enter Adrian's library find this hybrid array bewil-dering and do not pause to investigate it, preferring to stroll along the more familiar terrain to the left. So they are not aware that good old Adrian has collected occult wisdom over more years than any of them can remember, and that like a bee he distils a star-born nectar from many a mystic and seer. They simply enjoy the flavour of his port.

Adrian's book is the fruit of his study of sages and of himself. Carefully it is composed, and as carefully completed as far as it can go; each page attests to another day, another life of his inner being ... 'now'.

Now once again, Adrian bent over it, reflecting on his dilemma. "Shall I let this be read? Can my mite solve, or open to the world the Greater Mysteries? Would my contribution at this time of desperate emergency, be stillborn?" He fell yet again to wondering, "what is my knowledge anyway? Who can tell anyone else this thing as unseparate as the air I breathe and as impossible to grasp? Why, here it is all along, here it is, and only 'I' can find out." He got up stiffly to put another log on the fire and sat down again to thumb the beloved pages. His attention wandered somewhat, for it had been a long and concentrated day, apart from the visit to his tailor, and he was tired. The double life is a lonely one, but the heart beats in both chambers interdependently.

Yesterday he spent the evening with a colleague and old friend whose London pied à terre was a penthouse flat in the Barbican. After dining on delicate personal interests in their respective countries - for both men were trained to monitor psychological stress at summit level - he took his coffee and Armagnac, and went through one of the great picture-windows onto the wraparound balcony, to gaze down into the russet honeycombed space of the region by night. Illumined bridges and stairwells raised a net of covered walkways to the second storey podium, and linked a grid of towers and terraces with many eyes and many arches, to the central humming pulse of the concert hall and cinema complex, and to the incongruously soft grey stone of St Giles Church. Adrian had noticed on his way to the tower, that in the church they were performing that night, the *Song of Songs* set by the contemporary French composer Daniel-Lesur. He could just hear the splashing rain of fountains far below in the large rectangular ponds - or 'tanks' as he himself christened them, having travelled in India. He heard also in his mind, the footfalls of concert goers along the smooth geometrically paved galleries, and the festive voices of diners in the bright-lit brasserie.

He rolled the brandy round his tongue, and watched the destinies of tiny match-stick figures in this city within a city. From his elevated view, their motions seemed mechanical like pieces in a game, yet strangely confluent. Is his 'solace' of any use? Does not that same solace toil within those Lowry souls daily, producing and diluting seed, until it is taken neat? Few might brighten to the interior medicine, and they already know it for themselves; for most, who grasp the perverted form, it would depress and even destroy their lives.

Do they "want" it indeed? Is it not within them already?

In the quiet of his library Adrian gathered together the pages of his manuscript in one hand, and glanced at some statements, opened at random ...

> "There is," he read "an imaginary free will - to roam and to range and to form pictures of its own accord upon the screen which supports it ... magical cinematic, cyber space, made possible by light through projection ... molecular cohesion makes it possible to live ... the consequence of a man's action is ordained according to the reverberation of his previous action in other births, and to the Master whose composition he cannot know ...

12

"I am an instrument. I am free to be His instrument willingly! My freedom? My gesture turns at a right angle to what they told me ... My life evolves in a way that is perpendicular to the livelihood I was conditioned to 'imagine', and therefore I am revolutionary.

"Evolution submits; submission is Allah!

"I am the picture in a given frame. What other can I be? Who else am I? I act AS IF the conscious will is mine.

"Whose kiss awoke my sleep? ... I receive the intimate co-ordinance, as that One."

Pausing, Adrian looked up and gazed into the warm heart of the fire as into the sky. Some words came to him from the Rubaiyat of Omar Khayam, beloved since his boyhood:

"For in and out, above, about, below
'Tis nothing but a Magic Shadow-show
Play'd in a box whose Candle is the Sun
Round which we Phantom Figures come and go."

A strange shock of warmth seized him. It seemed to reach for him from beyond the core, the stem of his conception. He found himself asking "Pieces of paper? black-letter? who am I, then? if music be the food of Love, play on!" He read further in the manuscript:

"The higher Power is an inscrutable, collective, evolutionary purpose ... to bring the divine spark in everyman over innumerable lifetimes in different spheres of existence, back to his and her Source, as in the Sun."

At that moment, Adrian ceased to read and ponder, but stood

straight and tall. Some state described to him by a former teacher, entered him:

> *"When the Soul is saturated with light, Lightning strikes. 'S/he' quantum-leaps the Interval of the universe, and is no more separate. This semi-tone in a musical interval raises a third to a fourth, and a seventh to the octave resonance. From Seven tones of the rainbow is just one step to Eight, infinity's figure of pure light.*
>
> *"My end begins. My end cometh, without my comprehension, to crack the nut."*

He knew this not verbally. A shock throughout his being, dissolved the wall he knew, the shape he had been, the covers of his book, in a Song of flambent peace. What was this he held? Words - black letters on a surface whiter than ash - a mirror? "Is that my original face? The word is a boundary, a description, and my own I have lost."

Something from his open heart, the sky within space, imperiously beckoned him to make the connection into a flower's wide face: to leap. Deep in his breast it woke, glowed and hummed - in Nature's mirror it pulses to the left. It vibrated with power and strength, it shone like a lion. The manuscript fell from his hand into the middle of the fire place, where it was voraciously devoured by the flames. There are no accidents.

Every moment now, is this. Adrian sighed slowly, long and deep.

It called him and he is willing, as was the young Samuel, as was Daniel. The great Quest of his book, zealously pursued with argument, scholarly research and conscious experiential insight, is answered by the destiny he dared to probe and quicken. There is value in his offering. The radiance which now permeates him is white like a clear fresh spring; and now it expands. His duty to the world has changed its composition. Everyman must make a personal discovery in his and her own way, not by persuasion but in his or her time. Not all the buds on the Tree of Life open simultaneously. Eventually all will flower. The old man is warming his hands by the fire that now intensely burns from papers that can never be re-written. Looking into the lambent light as into stars, warm and bright, he smiles, he is perfectly at ease; for he has never, not for a long time now, disagreed with the Will of his destiny.

He half-recalls with joy the great lines of Dante which the teacher of Divinity in his schooldays used to quote, at morning assembly:

"In His Song abides my peace."

Excalibur

EXCALIBUR!

Silver gleam excelling, thrust into the rock of fate, hidden within dull grey stone, tarnished by the age, irremediable ... No man can see what shines within his fate, no man may remove its sting, the Sword which rules him from the rock, 'till as a boy he comes to back it, heart and soul, thorn of the Rose, his life. The boy alone was the sovereign the Sword awaited, for he wrestled not with it, used no sly sleight of mind to better it, but came as bid and lightly, effortless, drew it out and ruled his people. For the rock was the Water of Life frozen and now it flowed. The rock was the Water of Life that became a lake, the surface still and cool reflecting sky, and the hand of that lake gave unto him the Sword to hand, his kinship, so he was healed. And around his Table he formed his Company of Knights, and Chivalry became the gentle art of the land. A cheval they cleared the forest with steel and were stern with demons; within the heart, their path of love, they bowed to the lady Grace, their code of honour. And the Sword long dulled in the war of brothers of the land, recovered its polish, it gleamed, like fire it shone.

With Excalibur to my arm, how can I fail? Warm bright star in my heart, the mantle is but the rank outsider, and it is brown. Green and yellow are the colours of earth the Noble one, the current favourite ...

Phillip Molton awoke with a start and tried to remember his dream as it slid away back into the unknowing dark hill of the night. The strength of the dream, unlike any he had known before, illumined the chambers of his mind with some hidden message larger than life. Unable to sleep again, and striving to remember, his mind clutched and developed one tiny fragment, stepped down to his comprehension, metamorphic to a recognisable colour ... a horse it was, yes, a horse in his dream, and the colours of its jockey were yellow and green like the 'earth' wire in the plug, or buttercups of wet sunlight in the lush green grass of his garden. Never had he seen so beautiful a horse, a lively brown chestnut whose untold story warmed his heart: its name was Excalibur, and it had won easily. Yes - Phillip slowly spelled the image into his understanding - Excalibur was the winner.

But what was he, Phillip, doing on the racecourse? Cautious with all his belongings, he was no gambler. Occasionally he had permitted himself to flutter on the Derby or the Grand National, but he had gone no further for this than the betting shop on the corner, and nothing serious. The races? ... ah, noble creatures. Creatures of calibre.

Phillip Molton, to use his own words, was in 'dead trouble', and the bruising burden of this now flowed as fog into his dazed impression of the morning, and woke his woe. REDUNDANT. He'd been living on his redundancy money for many a month now, and there was no longer enough of it to make ends meet. Last year he was a supervisor in a pharmaceutical factory - producing a synthesised tropic 'booster' from chemical compounds - and it had seemed a safe position until it was taken over by an International group which declared him and others 'for the scrap heap'. He had applied for various positions in different firms, but at 55 was considered too old, and was by now utterly disheartened. His innate calibre was conditioned to his daily employment; the future looked bleak, and churned in his head. Although he lived alone, and so his tastes were not expensive, he had to pay the council tax and the building society and keep himself in food, shoes and such items as the TV, tools for the garden, and chatty magazines to pass the time.

He was in *dead trouble* because, as he dimly knew, he had not learned how to live, and time was running out. Very soon his benefits and savings would no longer cover him. He was loath to move, but tried to think of a way out. He concentrated on the situation, as a perceptive magazine article had advised him to do, but it simply made speeches about itself around and around his brain. No answer could be seen. There was no answer. His natural self-discipline forced him out of bed each morning to look at the exhausting desert of the day. Even the garden no longer engaged him. There was too much time to do everything in, and even that was running out. Aimlessly he whiled the hours, and was nothing but the passing, the passing away of that time.

This morning the force of the dream quickened in him some strange throb of colour. He heard himself saying "every cloud has a silver lining, sharp like steel" and wondered at the origin of this idea. A strange impression of warm vital sinews of Nature came with it; white wide light together with dark garments, seemed to fly as wings, as chords of blood and song. With a new interest he inspected his garden and did some overdue clearing around the azaleas. When he went out to get the groceries he passed by the betting-shop on the corner. Instinctively he stepped in.

"Tell me," he said, feeling his way around the thick cigarette of round-shouldered space to the counter, "is there a horse called Excalibur?"

The man behind the counter thought for a moment and consulted the form. "Excalibur ... Excalibur ... ah yes, here we are. Rank outsider. Never won a race. Not even placed, but he comes up tomorrow. Chepstow, 2.30. Want my advice? don't waste your money."

No, he wouldn't. Phillip left.

Chepstow! He would be there tomorrow. The power of that dream to see clearly ... he was a thinking man and had read about such things as *clairvoyance*: wasn't this happening to him? Today he had things to do.

By the end of the afternoon he had been to the bank to draw out his last savings, and to the pawnbroker with as much of his worldly values as he could carry and drag behind him. He succeeded in raising just over £1500. That evening he purchased some excellent take-away from the Bombay Palace that he had been recommended, and thoroughly enjoyed watching TV for the first time for weeks. It did not feel as if it were himself doing these things. When he went to bed he had no more dreams, but he felt he was dreaming anyway. Which way, by day or night, was 'real'? He had lost the distinction. Where would he wake up?

In the morning he entrained for Chepstow, travelling first-class in good time for the meeting. The racecourse was in full frenzied bustle when he arrived; three had already been run, the bookies were ticker-tacking the odds, and the crowd jostled at the barrier. He felt strangely at ease and detached, as if he entered the frame of a vibrant picture of his own creation, and moved among its urgent physiognomies and pungent equine odours. Some of these were so distant in the picture that he could pick them up between finger and thumb, and some of them so close they filled his sight and seemed to be of his own breathing. He preferred the Tote, as it seemed more trustworthy. To his astonishment he alone seemed to be space unmoving, as the energetic carnival danced around and through him, and yet he was now face to face with the Tote. On the board he saw in chalk: "EXCALIBUR - 100-1. Green and yellow colours." "Fifteen hundred to win on Excalibur," his voice said. The clerk gave him a long quizzical look and handed him a ticket for the 2.30, No.14 to win.

His feet took him to the bar, for a lager might now help things along, and to wait for the next race, due at 2.00. It was won by the favourite, whose unvarying favour he watched as from a great distance, tiny movements, and the crowd around him looked bored. Then he walked over to the paddock to see the saddling up. A very thin dark jockey in the colours of early summer leaf and golden buttercup was lightly tossed up onto No.14, a shining red-brown chestnut, just as he had been shown, who skipped and skittered coltishly on the muddy track, his quivering head firmly held by a bovine stable lad. The heart of Phillip swelled back into his spine with love for this noble, delicate creature of fire, for the tender web of its veins and sinew, its swishing tail and tawny legs like the strings of a violin. It was almost more than he could bear. He was afraid he might weep. Two bulky farmers behind him discussed the creature's points disparagingly. Excalibur.

Phillip did not want to watch the race. He found his way to the bar by the finishing-post so he could get a good view of the end. He gazed into his glass and pondered cheerfully "It *is* the dream. Zero to a hundred, the name of this great game all around, from standstill! Put your feet up, lay back and wait for the right job to come through. Hundred and fifty thousand. Hundred and fifty thousand back to the building society, not bad. No problem now," and enjoyed the enchantingly soft amber hue of his lager. Oh, Rose of my life.

The race had begun, and Excalibur was slow to start. Over the tannoy, the chatter of the commentator crescendo'd: "Torriano in the lead still, followed by Mercury, April Rain and then, well behind them, EX - calibur. Torriano looks all set to win, and Mercury is running well, April Rain dropping back, Excalibur coming up now on the inside, making a challenge, it's right on the rails, looks a bit rough just there ..." the commentator became excitedly emphatic "... this is between Torriano and Excalibur fighting it out, with Mercury in third place. It looks like a photo finish, it looks like Torriano with Excalibur second by a head, and Mercury third. Also ran were ..."

An entangled express-train of horseflesh thundered past the post, too fast for Phillip to see.

Like a stone his heart fell into his feet, rooted numbly side by side. The water of life may become a lake to drown in, brown in. The noise of the racecourse was a far-off twittering of songless birds, there was a roaring in his chest. But he loved the creature, so tawny gold of fire like a lion within him. *But he loved ...*

"Wait a minute," crackled the metallic tannoy "there is a Stewards' objection. New result for the 2.30. I repeat, new result. Because of jostling and riding-over on the rails, Torriano is disqualified. Excalibur is the winner and Mercury in second place, April Rain third. I repeat ..."

Phillip heard it all again, and was born again.

As one shy and retiring, modestly he handed over his ticket to the Tote pay-out clerk and put three hundred fifty-pound notes into his breast pocket without counting them, and began to whistle 'Lily Bolero'.

"I'll never have a dream like that again, honest to God! I promise. Those poor punters with their money on Torriano. The sky's Word is sharp like the Sword - hey, where did that come from?"

With a muttering of thunder the sky opened and it rained, sheets of rain fell. And he opened wide his arms and let it bathe him, silver gleam excelling, you had to hand it to him.

And then ....

A Cautionary Tale

From a Story by Graham Jacobs

EVERY DAY, Graydo was woken up at 7.30 in the morning, although not by his Mother or Father like most little boys. That duty fell to the family butler Hoskins. Hoskins would run the bath for Graydo, make sure his teeth were cleaned, and press his school uniform neatly, ready for the day's wear. At 8 o'clock the bells would ring for breakfast. As the house was so large, there were bells in every room, so when a meal was served everyone knew it was time to eat. The sound of bells for breakfast was rather like the dawn chorus. When it was time for lunch they sounded like bees humming, and at dinner time they sounded like a big steam ship blowing its horn.

Breakfast time was always the best meal of the day for Graydo, as he could tell his Mother and Father what he had dreamed about. But most of the time, Father would be eating his boiled egg and toast with his head buried in *The Times* and worrying about his money, whether the stock market had moved up or down.

One morning, Graydo did something most unusual. He asked a question. Normally he was not allowed to do this, as his Father thought that little boys should be seen and not heard.

"What is money, Father? Does it grow on trees?"

This must have irritated Father, because he showed his face from behind *The Times* and was about to say something, when Mother asked brightly "What did you dream about last night, Graydo?"

"I dreamt I was the King, and everyone was bringing me

presents for my birthday!

Point taken, thought his mother, it's nearly Graydo's birthday; but she kept her thoughts to herself, and told him to eat his breakfast – boiled egg with toasted soldiers, orange juice and a very nice cup of tea. He ate all this while reading his favourite comic, which had been ironed by Hoskins as the paperboy always crumpled it up when posting it through the letterbox with the other newspapers. Now it was time for school. The chauffeur was sitting in the Rolls Royce, ready to take Graydo to school and his Father to the office.

Graydo and his Father did not speak in the car, as they always played the News on the radio. This was all very boring for Graydo. On the way to school he looked out of the window to see if there were any larger houses than the one he lived in. At 9 o'clock he heard the pips: time for the News. He had to keep very, very quiet so his Father could listen, as it was so important. But that morning, during the News programme, Graydo asked his Father another question. This was a very dangerous thing to do, as last time he was ticked off severely. However, he asked, "Please Father, explain why if the stock market moves up you're happy, and if it moves down you're sad?"

For the first time, his Father was not angry with him. He thought this was rather an interesting question, from a nine year old boy. "Well Graydo, I am happy when the market moves up because we will have more money, which means we can go on living the way we do. But if the market goes down, then we might lose our money, and then we wouldn't be able to live the way we do."

"Oh, I see," said Graydo, pretending to understand, but he hadn't, at all. His Father patted him on the head and said "You will learn, my boy. Have a good day at school."

The school gates always seemed to Graydo to be so big. This gave him a scary feeling about school. But once inside, he would see all his friends and they would start to tell each other the best stories in the daily comic they all received, called *Cuthbertson Goes to Town*.

School started with Scripture, followed by English and Maths, a short break in the playground, and on with French and Latin. Latin was Graydo's worst subject. He could never pronounce the words correctly when his teacher Mr Maximus asked him to read out loud.

"Graydo, please read now."

"AM O ... AMA S.AMNUTI ..."

"No, no!" cried Mr Maximus "If you do not practice more, I will have to speak with your parents and ask them to stop your comic, as your school work is suffering. And believe me, you will need to work hard if you want to go to the same school as your Father did, and continue in his footsteps."

Graydo said nothing. He drooped his head on his desk. *RINGRINGRING!* Saved by the bell, and lunchtime. "Phew!" thought Graydo. Latin was not for him. Anyway, who needs to learn a silly old language from thousands of years ago which nobody ever uses, except in the chalky classroom with Mr Maximus. After lunch and the usual food fight which always got everyone into trouble, it was time for English with the Headmaster.

During this lesson, the class were discussing a story they had been told to read at home, when all of a sudden Graydo put up his hand: "Excuse me Sir! Can you please explain what happens when the stock market moves up and down?"

The Headmaster flew into a frenzy, threw his piece of chalk at Graydo and boomed "Get out boy, get out."

After the lesson, Graydo had to go to the Headmaster's office. He knocked. "Yes, come in," said the Headmaster. "Oh, it's our Graydo. Do you know why you are here, boy?"

"Well Sir, I suppose it is because I spoke out of turn when you were teaching, Sir."

"So what was the purpose of your question regarding the stock market moving up or down?"

"Well Sir, I asked my Father about this, and he said that when the stock market moved up we made more money so we could live like we do, and when the market moved down we lost the money. I really did not understand, so I thought where else better to ask than at school. After all, everyone tells me I come here to learn."

"That is all very well Graydo, but there is a time and a place. And English is not the time. However, I will satisfy your quest for knowledge. Now let me explain: you receive the comic *Cuthbertson Goes to Town* each day, don't you."

"Oh yes Sir, and it is ironed each day by Hoskins."

"Well, the people who make that comic receive money for selling it to boys like you."

"What is money, Sir?"

"Dear boy, they never let you find out! Well, money for the sake of this explanation, is like a pencil, see? Every day the comic you receive costs 4 pencils to buy. But it only costs 2 pencils to make the comic. What is 4 minus 2, Graydo?"

"2, Sir."

"Well, that is known as plus 2, the profit, 2 pencils."

"Oh, I see … "

"Now, when the company who makes the comic need some more pencils to make new and better comics, they need more pencils for that. So they offer part of their company to other people who can buy part of the company and give them the pencils. These people are known as shareholders. Now if the company is selling a lot of comics to children like you, and getting 2 pencils profit on each one, the value of the company goes up, and so the stock market goes up. But if the children stop buying the comic, the company can't get any pencils for profit. Then the market will move down."

"Well Sir, thank you very much for the most interesting lesson Sir. I think I am beginning to understand."

That evening, Graydo's Grandmother Ethel came for a visit. The bells rang like a steam boat, and dinner was served. During dinner, Graydo quietly explained to his Grandmother about pencil profit. She was so impressed that she decided to give him a present next time she saw him. When Grandmother Ethel returned at the weekend, she brought him his present – a £10 note – and opened his very own bank account for him to start saving. She told him that one thing was very important to remember. With the stock market you make money and lose money. Therefore you should always have some money in the bank, just in case things go wrong.

Graydo enjoyed his new found interest. He decided that from now on he would save money. This made him feel very grown up. His Father noticed him more, which made Graydo feel much more comfortable. So he asked his Father for some pocket money. His Father agreed, but on condition he wash his Mother's car every Saturday morning, for £5 each week. His Mother was not particularly happy about this, but never the less she agreed, as it might help Graydo in the future.

Over the years, Graydo saved every penny he could, and paid it straight into his bank account. By and by, he had lots of money saved. In the meantime, his school life continued, and seemed to improve as time went on. In his school reports which his Mother always read, it said "his Latin has improved, especially his reading."

"Well done," said his Mother "You really have improved at school. The reports say good things about you, and about what an attentive pupil and confident boy you are."

Time went on, and still Graydo was putting his money away, week after week after week.

One day, circumstances were about to change, most terribly. The stock market fell so much, that Graydo's Father lost all his money. "I am a ruined man!" he cried. Mother was very calm. She said, Surely everything is alright, we have money in the bank. But really his Father had put everything into the stock market and left nothing in the bank. "Never mind, it does not matter," said Mother confidently "we can sort this out."

"Mother, I have got money in the bank, we can use that!

"Oh no no, Graydo, that is your money!"

"But Mother, I had no use for it, I was just saving it, now I have one, I can help you and Father."

Tears rolled down his Mother's face. She was so proud of her son for his generous thoughts. And so Graydo gave his money to his Father, who was able to rebuild his money through some very wise decisions.

Graydo grew up, and continued to save. When he was an adult, he became a banker. He created special types of saving-accounts for children only; and when he got married, he taught his children to save.

The Kettle

RECENT RESEARCH into the papers of the late Reverend Lewis Dodgson, has turned up a lost and visionary manuscript, which he had intended to publish in Wonderland itself. It is entitled A Fine Kettle of Fish. *An extract from it so reads:*

Alice next came across a large river, or was it a stream? Perhaps half way between a river and a dream, she thought, as it certainly did stream. She was amazed to see, floating along in the Striver (as she had decided it should be called) a large open kettle in which sat, bolt upright, three large trout in grown-up clothing, paddling furiously against the strong brown current.

Nothing here in Wonderland should now astound her. Alice hurried down to the bank to take a closer look. Two of the trout were dressed as gentlemen and the other as a lady. They also wore labels: "NANNY MAGGOTY", "UNCLE GORBLIMY" and "UNCLE (SMOKED) SALMON". As Alice approached the flowing water, Nanny Maggoty called out imperiously, "Quick, save us! Pull the kettle out of the water *immediately*. We are floating downstream, out of control."

Alice was quick to obey, the tone of command reminded her of her own Nanny. "Don't worry, hold tight," she said and, grasping the great kettle by the handle, she pulled it out of the river and onto the grassy bank. "Thank *goodness* for that," declaimed Nanny, smoothing down her scales. "Now then. Who are YOU?"

"I'm Alice, and what are you all doing here?"

"Oh," said Nanny "we're a pretty kettle of fish. Mr Smoke

Salmon here is rushing away to safety, because he is being chased by a nasty bird with black feathers called Tollah, and I am taking him. But he should be leaping upstream, because that is his nature at the breeding season, as you know, anyway the current got the better of him, and he is taking us all down with him. Gorbie the Red Trout here, is supposed to be helping me, but he bumped his head and is bleeding."

Uncle Gorblimy, looking somewhat dazed, croaked out "Glas tnost Per resS troiker" in a loud and anguished voice, and used his paddle vigorously in the resistant river bank. Alice had never heard such words, and was nervous they might be bad ones.

All of a sudden, there was a loud chatter, and their company grew. A little bush squirrel and a curious Quail arrived onto the bank from nowhere.

"Who are you?" said Alice – she had got used to asking that question.

"Oh I'm just li'l Georgie, and this here is my Vice, Danny the Quail. Sure glad to meet you. Who're you, honey?"

"I am Alice! These three trout are 'scaping from an awful Tollah bird! You must help them. Can you tell me, Mr Squirrel please, what glasn ost and perresstro iker mean? He won't stop saying them and they might be bad words."

"Sure thing, sweetie. They mean 'Open the Door and Change Everything.'"

Danny the Quail nodded affirmatively, tugged at a large worm in the grass with his beak, and quacked, "Quark-quark! Three quarks for Mrs Mark! The meaning of life is ee-equals-em-cee-*Squarked.*"

"What about pie R squared?" said Alice intelligently, remembering her arithmetic lessons.

"Quark quark, it's apple pie! You want P, Q, blueberry or sweetie?"

Alice stamped her foot – "No, you silly old quark, Pie is 3.131459 recurring into infinity. You *know* that."

"Glas Nost …'

"Okay, that solves it. Pies are squares, squares are four, and twenty black birds quark, when they're baked in a pie. How many you want? QU …"

"Glas …

"SHUT UP, ALL OF YOU!" That was the unmistakable voice of Nanny. "Shut up *this instant*, be *quiet*, or I'll send for the Lord Chief Justice and have you all tried first and then locked up. We are trying to save smoked Salmon from an appalling Tollah, and green grow the rushes Oh. Who has a plan?"

There was total silence, and the Striver went on flowing, regardless.

Uncle Gorblimy was looking a bit better. His suggestions became more intelligible. "Why not write an open letter to *The Times*, *Isvestia* and *The Washington Post*? Everybody will read it, and save him. It'll change everything."

"No it won't," snapped Nanny. "That is not good enough. Fancy suggesting anything as wet, weak and spineless as that. The army wouldn't stand for it."

"Glas No st, Gla st Nos, O you woman of iron," crooned the red Trout admiringly in Russian. Uncle Salmon made one or two half-hearted leaps, but his heart wasn't in it, and the rest of the Company had come to a standstill. Georgie the bush squirrel got busy with the storage of his precious nuts. Danny the quail explored more black holes in the ground. The rest of them, Alice thought, looked like fish out of water.

All of a sudden there was a terrible flapping sound, and a dreadful Shadow fell over them. There alighted in their midst a very large bird wrapped in a blanket; it looked (to Alice) like a giant bustard. "Where's the infidel? And where's that maggoty old woman?" it croaked somberly. "War! War!" "Hiya Tollah, how're we doing there?" chirped Georgie. "Stop it, stop it," pleaded Alice, but everyone else laughed. "Here's the bill," said Nanny in her best form. "So WHO IS GOING TO PAY? There is only *one thing for us all* to do. Come on, all of you, get in a crocodile, that's it, file in and follow *me*. Here is a new song I wrote specially for this occasion. The refrain is "Here's a Fine Kettle of Fish" – it shouldn't be too difficult to learn. Come on, ALL OF YOU, give it everything you've got. We can't have any stragglers."

So Alice watched, astonished, as Nanny Maggoty, Uncle (smoked) Salmon, Uncle (red) Gorblimy, the Sinister Tollah, Georgie the Squirrel and his Vice, Danny the quarking Quail, with and without their conference-labels, all marched off after their pied piper along the river bank downstream in a long crocodile, singing more or less together:

"Let's all jump over the English channel
or dig underneath a Kentish tunnel.
Maybe the Economy will turn out
to be just the mouth of a wide open funnel

shrinking into Super space, with nowt
any more to shout. So what's our solution?
Red rev ruskie revolution?
Environ-mental de-poll-ution?
Another scandal convolution?
Here's a fine kettle of fish!
Let's all jump over the English channel
or dig underneath a Kentish tunnel,
to float the pound ..."

So singing, dancing, their voices fading, the Party disappeared cheerfully into the far distance. And Alice, alone by the river, could hear again the sound of the water. It certainly did stream and strive. "Curiouser and curiouser," she said to herself – "whatever next?" And she began to thread some daisies in her apron. They seemed to have taken their kettle with them.

To this manuscript, the Rev Dodgson had attached a memo:
"Sing merrily, life is but a dream.
But who is the dreamer?
And who is in the dream?"

The Book of Truth

THE CAFÉ Regis is still a favourite rendez-vous for the good and the great. The French Imperial décor conjures up a grandeur to satisfy those who fought hard to win and, like all conquerors, can relax only in the visible proof that the struggle is worth while.

Robert Marchant was a publisher. His *Lions Rampant* imprimateur was blocked in gold on many popular spines. As the founder and managing director of Leo Books plc, he was envied for his acumen, energy and skill in keeping afloat in a troubled market. He employed a network of personal friends and aides-de-camp as antennae.

One warm September day, Robert invited Laurie Meyer the poet, Flavia Marcus the feminist feature-writer and Bill Thompson his old school friend, to lunch with him. Bill was brilliant at research and could write reams on any topic you gave him, but had not a single creative idea of his own.

The purpose of the lunch, as of many others before, was to brainstorm next year's *Book of Truth* – one of a series. It should be the *fin-de-siècle* magnum opus! for Robert conducted his business with an old-fashioned flair and style which was discreetly coming back into mode. He invited Laurie the poet, because he liked him. Lauries's disheveled appearance, with studiously patched corduroys, shapeless jacket and wool woven tie, only just admitted him to the Regis. He was not hard up – the royalties from his collected works, lectures and readings were substantial. He projected a nonchalant pre-war Bloomsbury lifestyle – also becoming fashionable again. His boyish good looks and the unbrushed hair over his brow reminded everyone of the legendary Rupert Brooke.

"You're looking," he said, after they had all sat down to play with serviettes and silver and listen to Robert holding forth, "for the T-word. And that can be expressed only through the P-word. And that's only a beginning. If you want me to expand, I will."

Then there was Flavia, who had heard this remark several times. "So what does poetry really mean to you, Laurie?" she enquired sweetly. "And as for truth, I don't think it exists. It's entirely relative. Rain is the rain-coat maker's fortune and the sun-cream manufacturer's ruin. Well, isn't it?"

Robert looked at her, his eyes glinting with dislike, and wondered why he had invited her. Of course she was stimulating, and made a point of disagreeing with everybody, which gave many ideas a healthy kick-start. You needed someone to be the tester. He found her dark aquiline features, like an Italian model for a Modigliani, rather attractive, when enticingly encased in sensible costume, sensible shoes, sensible pearls. "Before you rush in to destroy everything my dear," he purred, "let's hear Bill."

"How should I know? said Bill, rolling bread pellets between his thumbs. "Give me a man who knows, and I'll write his story and interview him and read what he has to say, but if I don't know myself, who cares?"

Laurie reached to rescue the topic from banality. "I think Robert wants …" At that moment, the waiter arrived. The ritual was always the same. Robert ordered and everyone else ate according to his taste. "Yes, a little cold consommé first, and then the crown of lamb with mixed vegetables and a bottle of your Emilion. We'll see about the pudding later. Now, go on, Laurie?" Leaning across the tablecloth, his chin on one hand, he gazed straight into those laureate clear blue eyes. Everyone waited.

"The truth," said Laurie with quiet satisfaction "is, as Flavia says, purely relative unless – unless we are talking about absolute truth and nothing but. Is that what you really want, Robert? Because if it is, no one will buy the book. All the philosophical verbiage goes so far, but Joe public can, IF he wants the taste of nectar, which is doubtful, drink it only from a cup formed with artistry. Truth has an aesthetic ambiance, a flavour. The poet can come near it. The philosopher finds it jolly damn difficult."

"Oh come on, said Flavia, "Who says Josephine public wants nectar and not a double scotch on the rocks? Your abstract aesthetic ambiance won't wash, nowadays. It went out with the bathwater, oh … yonks ago. What about real life, what about passion and crisis and the drug culture and – and babies being born, what about death and torture and poverty and religious maniacs? You got your head in the sand, chum? Your own tiny greenhouse? Scotch on the rocks puts it mildly – a bloody mary, more like. If truth is to be tasteful, better let it *taste*. Yes that's my word on the subject – the F-word: Feelings. Flesh and blood. Here we all are, and that I do *feel*. Common sense. Only a thundering good novel can handle it. It's all a big question anyway, isn't it."

"All that stuff you talk about," remarked Laurie, "all that stuff is in *poet's* truth, triple distilled – you might say ninety-per-cent proof."

"Isn't it six of one and half a dozen of the other?" asked Bill, his voice slow and agreeable "I say, don't collect your eggs till they are laid. "

Robert said importantly "I want a great book – better than the last ones. The Millenium Book. Obviously it should be about truth, it should breathe, it should have plenty of wine and sex and good songs and death. It should instruct and entertain – otherwise it's not a commercial proposition – it should delight, enlighten and challenge. It needn't be dragged through the gutter, but it must sound the depths, to raise the glass. It's got to be politically sophisticated and politically neutral. And it can't cover stuff that's too arcane or specialist for universal appeal. It should have the common touch *and* the mark of gold on it. Well, get to work, you guys!"

"Wow," said Laurie tilting back his chair. "Got yourself a ghost writer then? Are we waiting for a miracle?"

"Robert will take the lion's share if the miracle happens," said Flavia wearily, and they all laughed, "But," she went on, "the old Midas has got the point. You've got to tap the unconscious to get results, to find genius. There you are, there's your theme. Find a theme for the Millenium, a really powerful symbol or metaphor, and build around it."

"You can't just pop down to the supermarket for it," objected Laurie, "genius doesn't work that way. We may be touching the sacred or the Shadow. Got to be rather careful."

"The sacred what … ?

"Probably," yawned Robert, his interest fading. "Anyway, I invited you all, to *sow the seed,* and now I shall have to wait to see who comes up with something? Don't tell me it can't be done!"

There followed a post-prandial pause.

Almost, you could feel the wool-like texture of this silence, and snip its fleece with shears. It lasted for a full two minutes. No one could speak, no word could form. In that interval, everybody seemed to know *what* had descended into their quietening, but could not say a word. This Book of the Millenium contained no pages to turn. It sang. It was nude.

At last, Laurie said "There's your answer, Robert."

"Oh hell, good heavens," said Robert who, with a leonine gesture had knocked over his cut crystal wine-glass. The burgundy stain pursued an amoeboid, angry shape on the white table linen. He growled at his guests, "That's enough for today, everybody. Let's enjoy the liqueurs with the pudding, if nothing else. Oh Bill, look after the damage for me will you? I think I am going to have to leave early."

"Do we have our coffee here, boys?" said Flavia richly "or is it a cup of tea in my place and a good laugh?"

"The lion," said Bill surprisingly "has always found it difficult to lie down with the lamb."

"Bitter Sweet"

The Madonna of Mabingdroth Wells

BETWEEN TWO wooded hills in mid Wales nestles Mabing-droth Wells, a little town which, at the time we have to tell, had forgotten the names of her dragons and lost the flavour of her waters. Situated on the border of Powys and Gwynedd and once a charming beauty spot, she was losing her youth to the big cities, her farmers to the Milk Marketing Board, and her looks to the inevitable eye-sores of municipal cosmetic development which encroach into the surrounding fields. Her water supply was now plumbed from the Alwen Reservoir, and the local brewer who had kept her merry was now no more; his sons had sold themselves to Courage Corporate. Few visitors now bothered to beat the track to her door. Her community, suffering from the dried-up sources of her grey-stone slate-roof parlours, her High Street supermarkets, her two chapels and one church, and the well itself which tasted bitter and could no longer be bottled, passed the time watching TV indoors and at the pub. And around Mabingdroth Wells the flowers came out in the summer and the sheep dropped their lambs in the winter, and nobody cared; nobody stared. The lady had endured the national change of life, and was no longer fertile. Only the surface was seen; to be driven through quickly.

In the taproom of the Red Dragon, Mike MacGrath, director of Tourism, and his municipal sidekick Evan, were seeking refuge. Mike cursed himself and the day he ever accepted the job of chief ponce. "What are we going to do?" he whinged over his second bitter. "We've tried everything to put this Godforsaken dump onto the map. You can't make silk purses out of an old sow, now can you?"

It was nearing high noon for Mike and Evan. They had been

summoned by the Town Clerk to a somewhat brusque interview. "Look here now, MacGrath. The council is fed up. Just fed up right to here. They are paying you zillions a year to boost tourism in this town and the result is sweet fanny zilch. If you don't jack up the figures this season, you're for voluntary redundancy boyo, sure as I'm the top banana round here, the chop, right?" With a benevolent leer, the Town Clerk made a graphic gesture across his lapels.

"Don't worry," Mike had said, "resourceful is me middle name, you leave it to me, I'll find a way, see if I don't. Goodbye for now." The heart within him sank like a stone. Jesus Christ. The sack. At a time like this. The mortgage and the car. Who'll ever employ him after this fiasco? Mike drank up and ordered the next round. Evan spoke in his high hill-farmers' falsetto, "indeed to goodness man, here's an idea for you, what about a sheep farmers' rodeo with Country music? That'll have them swarming here like a convoy of new age travellers."

"Piss off Evan. Only one thing will work here. We need a bloody miracle."

"You're bloody right, Mike. I know. What about finding a dinosaur's footprint?"

"Not big enough, punk. Try harder."

"What about finding the house," Evan pressed the side of his nose conspiratorially "where Uther Pendragon stayed the night Arthur was - you know?" Left hand thumb and fingers made a suggestive ring around the forefinger of his right.

"Corny, man. Something bigger please."

"What about Owen Glendower's headstone where he rested on the retreat from the English brutes?"

"Every town around here has flogged Glendower's hair oil and the vile spa water which is poison to drink. No, Evan boyo, we're up shit's creek without so much as a paddle unless you can think of an idea, fast. Get moving lad, or else I'll be kebab'd by that bastard of a town clerk and you with me, laddie."

The barman had been listening to their conversation while he dried glasses and stacked them on the shelf above him. "Got to get it flowing, boys. Something has to. God, this stuff we get to drink nowadays, enough to make you weep. Got a drop of the old ale in the barrel here, if you fancy...? Ah thanks, don't mind if I do." He poured three good creamy heads, and they ruminated companionably in the nutty brown depths, but without inspiration. All the dragons, devils and green men in the district had been nabbed and were being milked for all they were worth. Owen Glendower, the liberator of Wild Wales, was resting in so many places, he had fallen fast sleep. The whereabouts of Camelot continued to be contested with Glastonbury. Oh for the rumoured powers of preacher-prophet Huw Lloyd for raising the dead! But he, so the story had it, had thrown all his necromantic books into the Llyn Pont Rhydden below Ffestiniogg before he died, and a mysterious faery hand had arisen from the waters and taken them all, and that was that. Back there in the seventeenth century, the exigent tourist industry was not so much as a bad dream. If our Mabingdroth Wells was Queen Mab of the Faeries herself, she had nothing to show for it except the scarlet poppies in her fields of summer hay, and the dawn chorus through white stems of silver birch, and these are things that can be neither fed nor sold to the commercial undertaker.

What is the difference, they asked, between "entrepreneur" and "undertaker"? The question remained unanswered. The ambiance of the Red Dragon itself began to supply some life-blood to their musings. Why are Welsh dragons said to dislike the colour red? A winged serpent once bathed high up in the Pistyll Rhaedr, the highest fall of water in Wales, and ate people. A stone pillar studded with iron spikes and draped with a scarlet cloth was placed by the falls, to enrage the dragon's appetite; so he dashed himself against it, ate his own blood and died. Like to like, as red rag or rage to a bull the dragon devours its own tail. Round and round they go, the problem fixed. Three men in the bar are talking worldly matters; but subtle currents play through their heads and over their dead bodies. A giant yew-tree in Nevern churchyard oozes a natural red resinous discharge: food for thought. What is the build-up of such things? I heard tell of a stone lion somewhere in a french market place, from whose mouth bright dew falls gently, even on the hottest summer day. Cracks in concrete behind the stone lion may accumulate concealed condensations of rainfall over the years; this reservoir is the apparent source. Things are produced as a miracle or as a birth, from the gathering of a tendency until it has no alternative but to break through. All these tales have been nabbed by other towns, but not one of them has been Mabbed. The pen-dragon is dry. Drinkup time. In the street outside, poor epileptic Hugh, the local idiot, lumbered by, untunefully singing. In the bar of the Red Dragon as the afternoon wore on, the Celtic Mystery declined into deepest twilight.

* * *

That night, Evan Evans lay awake in his cottage and remembred what Mike had said about needing a bloody miracle. A really bloody one. Isn't there a ...? Got it! He'll fix it. Fix it. For a girl called Caitlin came to mind from bygone summers, and with her, a certain little dell in the wood not far from his house; and a connection was made. The pendragon began to do joined-up writing; for Evan is by trade a plumber, the best in the town to marry the male to the female copper pipe under the sink, and spring the leak.

The following morning, having paced out the yardage and checked his supplies, Evan got on the phone to Mike and unveiled his plan. "Look you here Mike? You said what we need is a miracle? How about this. You pin your ears back now. We get daft Hugh to find a relic of this Carmelite nun in the field behind the municipal carpark, see? - yes, chapel won't like it very much, but we want the novelty here you see - where can you get a clay woman with a bit of a hollow inside her - shut up Mike - yes the Carmelite monastery back of Stony Lane, yes, got that - well if you can find one for me, I'll fix her on a pedestal, plumb her into the red-oxide spring in the dingle, and tears of blood will come out of her eyes whenever I turn on the fucking stopcock!"

"Evan you old lunatic, you'd better come on over."

Mike looked hard at his faithful aide-de-camp arriving breathlessly. He grinned. "Laddie," he said, hitting him on the shoulder "you're a bloody genius. I think you've solved it. Tonight boyo, start digging. In that ruined convent there's a clay Madonna, we've been storing it for Sothebys. Get a long hose this afternoon, but make sure you don't get it in this town, sink it and run it to the red oxide stream. Then put all the topsoil grass back nice and tidy. Mum's the word you old son of a bitch. Oh Christ this is great. I'll sugar up Hughie and then prime up the press ferret. He'll do anything for beer money. Son of a gun!"

After dark, when the town had gone to bed, the two men met in the field between the municipal carpark and Evan Evans's cottage, to assemble the private parts of their conspiracy and lay its serpentine current along the ground. The operation took some nights to complete, as turf replacement tactics had to be accomplished before dawn, to reveal a pristine field disturbed by nothing but sheep and Farmer Price's heifers. With steady stealth, the Mabingdroth dragon entered the earth as the coppery glint was plumbed to the hose-pipe both ends, wedded and embedded at the cost of muffled curses and of dark circles under the eyes of the director of Tourism at the Town Clerk's office, which did not go unnoticed. "Get your pecker out of that hole," he was told, in no uncertain terms. "If you don't get a move-on and show me a sheet of figures by Monday you get the chop, and you don't get no ceevee from me neither."

The Madonna herself presented a few technical problems. Though fired, her clay was somewhat porous, with cracks here and there. It seemed likely that the pump-room in the red-oxide dingle might cause her not so much to weep as to perspire rather copiously all over. Evan and Mike felt that this was not in good taste. They worked hard to shore up some pores with cement and artfully encourage others. In due course they achieved a somewhat ravished effect, which would have to do. The tears need not be produced round the clock: if they were, the conception might embarrassingly disintegrate. It made sense to regulate the seepage to a few well-publicised moments at traditional intervals of holy office. Some further pipe was laid through the field to Evan's bedroom, to provide one of these at the monastic dawn hour. Give the lady a break - why should she cry all day? There's a Union rule against it. Her exterior was carefully abraded in some areas, and patched and polished in others, with mud, sand and water from the stream.

* * *

On Friday, the news hit the media. A wandering mystic, young

Hugh Rhys-Evans, had stumbled on a statue half buried in a field at Mabingdroth Wells. Upon Hugh's investigation she wept tears of blood. Poor Hugh was discovered shortly after, lying in the grass with his tongue bitten quite through, but here was truly an awe inspiring sight. Professor Morgan Griffith-Williams of the Llanidloes History Society verified that the ruined Carmelite monastery nearby had once sheltered a Saint Brione in the Middle Ages. This must be her ruined statue, said to be possessed of a deposit of miraculous virtues, but never until now located. Dr. Owen Isaacs of Newtown tested the droplets that ran down her cheeks and found them compatible with samples of blood plasma that several centuries had rusticated. A team of dowsers arrived from London's Research Into Lost Knowledge Organisation, and confirmed that here at this very spot, a telluric ganglion pulsates. Their instruments both subtle and gross, responded briskly over other parts of the field as well, and the whole region around Mabingdroth Wells was declared a super-convergence of leylines whose loose ends were hitherto unresolved.

It was as if a dam or obstruction had been removed. A concealed and till now flaccid corpuscle of Mother Earth began to flow and glow with occult life. Her hidden nervous netting among the innocuous woodlands and sour meadows brought atmospheric disturbances. Notices and signposts were hastily designed, and a protective fence installed around the enigmatic Madonna, a stranger to these very parts. Reporters, photographers and Evan's convoy of New Age travellers began to besiege Mabingdroth Wells with traffic, marijuana and tents. The pub filled, a new sandwich bar opened, and problems of litter and drainage began. Mike MacGrath chaired the press conference. Hugh Rhys-Evans was alas able only to stutter inanely through a brace of stitches on his tongue, but the rest of the team were calmly confident. The lilt of their excitement and the pallor of their ravaged faces from loss of sleep, bore witness to matters beyond rationale. The media stood convinced. The story broke, nation wide.

It worked like giving pork to rats. That weekend, thousands flocked to the little town, and there was talk of a Celtic Lourdes. Poor bewildered Hugh received more attention than he had ever known in his life, and was shown his picture in the papers, but was still unable to articulate his mystic vision. The chapel minister chatted with Roman papists face to face. The few hotels being booked out, the town received a sudden and untaxed cash influx of paying guests and provisions for improvised bed and breakfast. There was talk of opening another campsite in Farmer Griffith's thistle field. Tourism escalated beyond record.

Evan Evans stowed away and turned his little tap. A large crowd gathered, jostled and laid bets. Presently, one of the mute eyes of the madonna of earth and clay could be seen to shine. It quickened to sunrise as a drop of dew. Soon a bloodshot tear formed in her other eye; then more gathered, to roll down her face, welling also from her heart. There was silence. Some were terrified. The effect was unpremeditated. Some turned away, some snapped her on their phones, or fell on their knees. A number of rosaries appeared. Others gaped or cried "Look, more! more!" "It is her sign," said one "for Armaggedon and climate change." "Our Lady of Sorrows," said another. A camera team from Channel Four verified it all. The Town Clerk nudged Mike. "Well, look who's the lucky sod then. I think you've got yourself saved." A brisk picture-postcard industry was born.

All went well until one day a crestfallen Evan entered Mike's office.

"We've been shopped," he burbled. "That meddling Vivian

Davies-Mogg, the schoolmaster. You know he asked those snoopy kind of questions? Well he took his class for nature study in the dingle, and the kids found the hose, he's traced it. In the stream. Mr Price's field. He's told the Mabingdroth gazette. We're for the big ride, Mike. The shit has hit the fan. Sky high, indeed to goodness."

Mike slumped. What is it to be - arsenic, the hose from the car exhaust to the bedroom, the railway track, or should he run for it? Bloody, bleeding *hell*.

Then a weak voice leaned hesitantly round the door. It was Megan Jones, the cleaner. "Mr MacGrath. Please. May I speak with." For a brief moment the two men forgot their problem and helped her sit down to get her breath. "It's my Gwyn-nedd," the lady was saying, rocking herself and cutching Mike's hand, "my Gwyn-nedd has come over strange. My Gwyn-nedd has had a vis-ion of the Mad-onna from the Carm-elite mon-ast-ery."

MacGrath had his head in the noose, it could go no further. So nothing now mattered. And he forgot what he'd been brought up to scoff. He put his arm around Megan and said to her, "Let's all go and see her, dearie."

* * *

They walked to Megan's old stone cottage in the meadow of ox-eye daisies. Evan and Mike both had to support the frightened cleaning lady. They opened the gate and crossed the field of dancing wild white stars in deep green grass, by the beaten path, and entered the cottage by the kitchen door. A deep silence, seeming to sing, in its turn entered them, sharp and sweet in motes of sunlight that played within the walls , with the indeterminate yet vivid flavour a bee may find in a flower. Manna is soft on the ground, like dewy white mushrooms at night. It made them dizzy. Here on the uneven stone flagged floor by the old cooking range, young Gwynedd knelt, her eyes open wide. "She's been like this for hours," whispered Megan. "She won't move. She won't hear me."

The young girl's black curly hair spilled from the gaudy plastic clip which fastened it. Her spine was a vibrant beech stem, her hands lay open to each side. The visitors to the low-ceilinged room at first stood awkwardly, looking around. In spite of themselves, they lost their power of thought, that small snide outcast. The power of the embrace gathered them in. Nobody could move. A fly buzzed on the window pane a long way off. Light entered the little room with the sun, but the radiance had another source. Like milk it filled the room. Like fire it streamed from the young girl and burst within the chrysalid of her watchers.

The eye is only a well, and who can say where that comes from? So nothing is seen, yet all of it fills; as the butterfly in every point of space alights. Her face is tender like the sap that rises in young flowers, motionless as primaeval granite, and open as a newborn baby. She is drowned in the dancer of her being.

Without knowing how, Mike found himself on his knees. Something seemed to have pushed him down. He dimly heard Evan mutter "...boy-bach" and Megan catch her breath. Whiteness rang and rang without a sound, and soundly dunked them all; they lost the face and form of who they were. "She won't stop," trembled Megan "my God, she won't stop ..." She longed to rest, but Gwynedd wouldn't let her. It shone from the kneeling girl onto the white-washed kitchen wall and window. Inexplicably, these reflected back, virgin ripe, face of arcane beauty - no mere image on a surrounding veil, but height, depth, the breath ineffably born. Yet you can pass through it your hand, for it weaves a hologram, cross-beams of the light, a universal tapestry. It is lodged in the being. It shimmers.

The play is deeply inward. Those eyes bestowed upon Gwynnedd, Mike, Megan and Evan their bounty, pulverising as between transparent plums, all separate ideas of themselves.

From the eyes of the Madonna of Mabingdroth Wells were born bright beads of dew. They formed from depth the stars, songs, then worlds - at dawn they are ruby red, like poppies circling night, scarlet as shy pimpernel, deep as the rose whose perfume fills the room. They welled, they fell from the womb of life, the Mother, the seed. They flowed in the heart.

The Dreamer within the Dream

ONCE UPON a time, there lived in a very large city a chartered accountant called Jeremy Montfort. Like most of the millions of human beings - of whose existence he was habitually aware, partly through hearsay and partly because he could see for himself - who inhabited this very large city, Jeremy lived entirely alone inside a train of thought. Knowing only that he had been born to inhabit this train all by himself, with his own parents, brothers, Aunt Mavis, friends, ex-wife and a sprinkling of persons he disliked looking into his windows, Jeremy had no idea where this train was going, or from whence it had begun its journey. Occasionally when a child, the thought had hit him and made him dizzy.

Although Jeremy was so used to travelling in a train that he never thought twice about it, he had since the age of twenty-nine a phobia about *railways*. This was due to a disturbingly clair-voyant dream he had had. In his dream he lay comfortably asleep across the rails of a section of railway track at the top of a steep hill that arose from the bowels of the city. For some strange reason he had no intention of moving from this spot. He was confident that any locomotive leaving the terminus below and accomplishing the difficult gradient would, on seeing him lying there, lose heart and steam and roll straight back down the hill again. This indeed proved to be the case. He heard a number of trains which strained to approach, took a look, gave up and receded. And Jeremy Montfort slept on, triumphantly unmolested upon his hilltop. He had also once heard "It cannot avoid you by leaving the rails." And this he knew, a train no matter how hard it tried, could never do. It must roll back where it came from. In this manner, time passed.

One day, the rails began to vibrate and clatter, and he became aware that a passenger-train was climbing the hill with unusual determination. He was reminded of the old fairytale, in which princes from all parts of the land strove to gallop up a sheer hillside of shining glass, to claim the bride who sat enthroned upon the summit; but he had never thought of himself in that way. He could now hear the complaining voice of the engine clearly:

"Thistrainrunsonwoodensleepers, thistrainrunsonwoodensleepers, you'rethickastwoplanks, you'rethickastwoplanks, watchoutyou'll-gethit, watchoutyou'llgethit, you'llgethit, you'llgethit, YOU'LL-GETHIT, GETIT, GETIT," and with a deafening clanking crescendo and a searing scream - his own - the great iron wheels neatly severed his head and his feet with a blinding flash of steel.

* * *

This nightmare, unlike those of his childhood, did not decently fade. Jeremy found himself henceforth prone to a strange irrationality, which would have filled his younger train-spotting persona with disbelief - *he was afraid of trains*. He was able to travel in one, with the help of a stiff drink or two, but he could not bear the sight of those gleaming parallel lines, and to cross a railway line by bridge brought on an attack of appalling dizziness, making him sick. This greatly restricted his movements in life. He sought help unsuccessfully from a hypnotherapist, a behavioural technician, and even his local Vicar. Fortunately he was good at figures and at handling Company law, and was able through persistent hard work to build up his accountancy practice from home, to travel when he had to, by bus, and to avoid all railways like the plague.

One day, an emergency arose. He received a letter by the morning's post from his elderly aunt Mavis who lived in

Sheffield, informing him that she was coming to visit him to discuss her Will, and would be arriving at Kings Cross on the midday train, and would appreciate being met, as she was unable to find her way around in the big smoke. Aunt Mavis at ninety-four was obstinately not on the telephone, and her eyes had seen better days. She seemed to be fond of him; her late husband had covered himself from head to foot with insurance on Jeremy's recommendation, and left her a packet. It made sense to continue to play his cards right with the old girl. Jeremy cursed, primed his gut with a fog of double-Scotches and took a taxi to the station. It was some time since there had been 'an emergency', and Jeremy Montfort who was not a habitual drinker, was merrily the worse for wear by the time he paid off the driver. Unsteadily he plodded across the station concourse; several people and unidentifiable metal objects bumped into him without looking where they were going. "Shober up, shober up," he told himself, and straightened his tie and shook his head to clear it. There was a very large number of people on the platform to meet the train, and he never knew quite what happened. It is known that his aunt Mavis had a fatal heart-attack on the spot, and that her Will remained contested.

* * *

In some indeterminate region of time and space, Jeremy Montfort became aware, from (it seemed) a great distance but may have been only a few feet or centimetres, that he was watching a body, the one he used to inhabit, and with some threads of life still in it, being carried to hospital in an ambulance. As the body gave up the ghost, his consciousness became suddenly and unrecognisably illumined with a disturbing question - "Who am I? What is this? When? Where? Why?" An agonising vertigo drowned him as instantaneously he existed in all places and all times, and in no individual form, as measureless endless space for ever and ever. In this, he was not even a speck. And even this non-entity, as a vaccuum, burned and burned and was conscious.

A great trough of darkness beyond all bank of memory intervened.

At some point there came an awareness of infinitesimal motion *swimming* along a tunnel with no walls. It couldn't be birth, for there was nothing to enclose it. Some unidentifiable faculty of vision seemed to seek refuge in a clarifying of the abyss which drew near. This gave the fiery question which continued to consume all definition, a peaceful focus. A small, still light at the centre of the flame, did not burn, but *received* his question. Presently there was no tunnel but light, the compass of all and everything. The consciousness which had been Jeremy Montfort, though disembodied, now occupied again a train of thought, and was rescued as if from the ocean onto a beach, by a kindly luminousity of itself. "Rest for a while now," came an unknown but familiar voice "and then we will talk about the beginning of your life."

He who had been Jeremy, was not now a body, but *he knew himself*. The resting consciousness does not struggle to arrest itself. As a dim light, this awareness hovered throughout a term of infinity, in which time and space took no form. It might be best described as a semi colon from which no train of thought continues, just a wide white space to the end of the line. But this space is without end. If you look into it, it is blank and yet alive. The I-consciousness or he who had been Jeremy, remained aware but without memory, and thus carefree; and we shall continue to refer to this semi-comatose 'eye' as 'Jeremy'.

In the kindly and limitless glow of light, the quiet voice

continued to inform him:

"Well Jeremy, you have had a good rest. I am going to talk to you colloquially in language you will understand. We always do, here. Do you know who I am?

"Air. Ariel. A real … What am I, and where are we?"

"For the time being, regard me as your 'spirit guide' to lead you on, and to receive your question. At this moment you are on a certain plane of being. It is called - for want of a better word, or should I say *world* - 'limbo'. For our purpose this word 'limbo' comes from the medieval latin phrase *'limbus fatuorum.'* This is the post mortem abiding place for fools and halfwits. One who lies across his line of fate and sleeps, is considered 'irresponsible'. This means he is incapable of responding to his subconscious, and would be unable to recognise heaven or hell as a reality. I have to say that you keep company with a vast multitude of other sleepers along the line, but you cannot see them because you do not think laterally. However, you do possess the vertical faculty of *awareness*, however dormant, and so you get hit. There is no limit to the fact of awareness. It contains the seeds to awaken. So we can work on this *awareness* itself, for your spiritual development.

"Now, you have a choice, regarding spiritual development. First of all, I am going to outline a few elementary possibilities. You may then decide how you think and feel about them. These possibilities are forms or vehicles of thought, which take root in mind-space and pursue a destination or world-space. Strong attachment or attraction to any one of these, may manifest as a lifetime or body in the world-space, such as that from which you have just woken. Equally, such thought-forms can be dissolved before they precipitate into chronological space. As the way of the mind, several or a multitude of these may exist concurrently. There really is no limit to awareness, or to the instant of perception it can expose and enter, as a living vehicle of the Universe. The choice is yours, to find out what matters of importance lead you and entrain you. I am simply here to help you to illumine your field. Remember, each image that arises is of air. It is will o'the wisp. It can enclose you in a birth only if you fall asleep inside it. Come, let us look at the field!"

In his un-bordered clarity of consciousness, Jeremy was able to follow the gist of this. "The field" of which his guide spoke was a misty and attractive settlement of twilight, like the surface of a frameless painting. Containing within it the entire potential of height and depth as sky to abyss, he found that filaments of light therein were born, as if from nowhere, and likewise expired. Like glow-worms they seemed to form spirals or tiny coils of static electricity, moved slowly in the horizontal 'fabric' of the mist as among long grass, and disappeared. They were sweet and homely, like - the thought came to him - the lights of a city or lone house, from an airplane or hilltop. This thought then disappeared. But Jeremy knew from somewhere that this field is 'his body'. He knew this within the awe and immensity of the great night. Something in this night arose in him with imperious power - a new question: "What? Where? Who AM? ..." an agony to resolve. It burned. It burned like the violet core of a flame, beseechingly. It yearned, it burned, it longed to take root. Every home it built for itself fell down because a train ran into it. None of it would stand up. Who are these ... *rooms*? Not one of them is true! All of them are uniquely the One room and yet all are distinct. His spirit guttered. The body decomposed.

"Witness," his spirit guide went on, "the end of the beginning. Each and every one of those glowing little filaments is a 'possibility'. In the pocket of earth time, these are assumed as lifetimes, as incarnations, as *embodiments*. In each of these is recorded as a thread, the entire tapestry of human history and its planet, beginningless, endless. But they are made out of light, the stuff dreams are made of. Out, brief candle! another is lit. The fiery seed, the flame itself, has no perception of time. All candles of many colours are the same to the fire that drinks the wick. Now then! At this stage it is our task to find out what choice you have, for your development. The essential question you have asked, the quest of *awareness*, begins to search into your being. This means you are no longer asleep. First, we must consider the costumes and rituals of this question which lie uppermost. In your receding earthly embodiment, you handled the accounts of others quite ably, but not your own. So you were called *an accountant,* and are now called to account, are you not?"

Jeremy nodded. He was beginning to see descriptions.

"You could not then see your own account, how it lay on the line," continued Ariel. "Now, to develop from there, we can make you into anyone you like. The possibilities are infinite. Firstly, as part of this rehabilitation questionnaire, you must answer whether you wish to be born as a human being, and whether you wish to be male or female. Once you've reached this point in the affirmative, we will not allow you to descend to the animal kingdom. Believe it or not, your own question shows you have already passed beyond that. Next, you need to decide which historical century you wish to be born in. We are not to be bothered about time, for your coming incarnation; in your case you may go forwards or back in time as we please, for in the context of the soul's spiritual development, all time is space, and exists instantaneously. You have reached a stage in which a momentum is disrupted; continuity is a laterally extending concept. So you may be a cave-man, a vestal virgin, a cabin-boy on the Golden Hind, a Maharani in a medieval indian state, a farmer in tsarist Siberia, an astronaut in the year 2040 ... whatever you fancy."

Jeremy knew an all-too-familiar vertigo where his head used to be.

"You may," his advisor went on "prefer to go to another planet altogether. That in itself is so immense a possibility, we do not attempt to answer it until we have decided whether you wish to return to Earth as it's called, or not. Now, on Earth there is plenty to wear, and to keep you busy. Would you like to be a fool? or a genius? or both at once? - they often are, you know! What about a circus clown, or a millionaire who starts in rags and ends in riches, or a millionaire who loses everything and ends in rags? You could be a curate if you like, or a teacher, or a neurotic, or - as they say on old Earth - *rich man, poor man, beggar man, thief; doctor, lawyer or Indian chief.* How about being a queen or a president for a change? Why not a great opera-singer, great actor, international sportsman, train robber or *even* - such a strange and novel occupation - a *writer*? Why not stay a child? Our discussion could go on for ever. Which nationality, which faith would you choose? why this one and not that? Remember, it's your life you are considering. Now, reflect awhile! I will return when you call me."

Poor Jeremy, alone again as immensity, felt ill, astounded and confounded. The varieties of probability collided with his shrinking status from all angles. Choose to be anybody you like! Decide what life you would like next! Who was he, *where was he*, to make a decision like that, to plan a life from womb to tomb? when innumerable detailed factors of every moment were involved. Account-keeping for a web of unique and intercon-necting lives threatened to drown him. And what, in 'limbo's' name in all this, was meant by 'spiritual development'?

"Well," he said to himself, after prolonged musings, "I suppose I would like to help others to put their accounts straight. But how can I if I can't balance my own books? How can I ever respond, not knowing past or future, to what's best for *me*? Who am I really, really? If I just knew that, I could be content. If I create anything without knowing this, something could go badly wrong. All sorts of peoples' *lives* are involved. No," he replied firmly to a childhood ambition, "I can't possibly be a train-driver. You know that. I might run someone over. Those trains are terribly hard to stop."

In ethereal turmoil, Jeremy called out "Ariel! Spirit guide! where are you? I give up. I can't. You decide for me if it is to be Earth. I don't know what's best for me. What's my spiritual development? please explain." At the same moment, Jeremy identified with clarity his ruling mental mode: it was *fear*. And he suffered.

Through the battering of gigantic and remorseless wheels he heard again the quiet voice of his guide; and the spinning, the dislocation of his universe subsided.

"Yes," Ariel was saying, silvery toned from a distance, coming closer, "that is exactly what everyone says in the end. You have to be challenged to see that it involves a bit more than choosing sweets from a plate. It is one of our tests to meet. We alone can decide what is best for you in the context of everything interconnecting, as now you see. We alone are able to see the entire course of your past and future lives from watershed to ocean, NOW. Nor are we the creator of your destiny. One day, you will know who is. However, from the standpoint of observation, we know you better than you know yourself - which in your case is very little - and can offer some guidance. It is all a play of light you understand - a *dream* ... and it is unavoidable until you learn to be the *willing* dreamer. Along those lines of conduct, we can help you. We," the guide hinted mysteriously "are *all of you*. We are in the centre of your lake."

"Wait a minute," said Jeremy *"why do I have to be born at all? Why can't I just stay like this?"*

"Ah!" said Ariel "we're getting warmer. Perhaps it may help the suicidal sleeper on the line, to remind him of a certain great fiery question. Yes? Well now, a simple explanation is that fire has a raging thirst! for *life*. Fire, as the Upanishad says, is latent in the wood, as cream within the milk. Fire and Water have been wed in all the ancient mythologies. The thirst in the fire, is to realise its own true pure Source. It cannot do that until it has burnt up every vestige of carbon - the action of lifetimes, the fuel - thrown onto it. When all which obscures is gone, the Fire re-enters its natural state of clarity which is *awareness*, invisible yet immanent in *all* things. Until then, its latency, flammable in all things as in the wood, is a boundless insatiable feeder, and forces birth. The thirst is in the fire. The fire enters even the lake; for the lake, calm and still, is the ultimate nature of the fire."

"Well," said Jeremy, "I need a while to take that in. Could you tell me about other worlds, as well as this kindly Limbo here?"

"All in good time," replied Ariel. "First, let us return to the question of the lines of conduct. We have ascertained so far that you wish to be of service to others. This in short, means you desire to widen your perspective and discover fellowship; you cannot however, be of any help to others until you *are aware of your self*. You also wish to let me make the decisions for your management, once I have conferred with my colleagues as to what will be best for you. Well and good! You survived the temptation to enter a persona of worldly glamour and lustre, for which I congratulate you, for such persons produce a pile of fossil-fuel which takes many lives to burn up. Now rest for a while. I'll be back with more information."

* * *

Left alone again, the ethereal swirl that was Jeremy floated, a little galaxy in unbounded space as if in the almost motherly arms of something that knew him. For now he trusted, and discovered that he could abandon himself to Reality, and let himself be permeated by its *absence* of time. And so he rested, and so he knew his renewal, the sacred force of Love, the arousal from nothing, of substance to kiss the flame. When he was all consumed in the no-thing which held him so graciously, something in him began to expand and be contained, like a pin of fire into a socket of earth; and he adored God and knew his evolving consciousness is male, through all its forest of forms.

Then Ariel, the harbinger of his knowledge, returned to him. "Well, so you want to know more about Earth?"

"Yes," replied Jeremy, "that would be helpful."

"I can tell you a little, which may be of use to you in your present state of the ground. You realise don't you, that though you are in this ethereal element here and now, self-realised, and have knowledge, that is not the case in the birth you are about to take. You are aware there are many fields to plough and much wood to burn. To live in time is very different from living in infinite capacity for awareness. In awareness however, you have surrendered to "thy Will be done", and so it shall be, through knots and clods of progress. You see, though each and every Soul is the root, the stem of Unity, the One, each branch makes for itself a different-seeming destiny towards realisation, with different views. Only the observer, seeing the whole tree of Life, sees truth, and only each branch becoming inwardly *aware* as it grows, recognises its Self in the stem, which is the same. And so we, in the briefing of each birth, can give it only the *aspect* of truth it is likely to see. You follow?"

"Yes, of course," said Jeremy.

"Now," went on Ariel, "in Earth you are very ignorant. You lay across the line of truth, and it came up from under, and hit you. Get it?"

Jeremy shuddered.

"This needs to be fully realised through recurrence," said Ariel. "Your reaction makes this plain. Remember: the dimension of truth rises at a perpendicular to the dimension of the known. The known on Earth is merely its cross-section. The tree of your life and realisation rises through the horizontal plane of your nescient Earth. Sleeper awake, and carry the cross! Of this, you need more experience. So I am now going to tell you only what is relevant to your cultural plane of experience.

"The planet or plane of Earth is on the fringe of a huge wheel or galaxy, a long distance in space and time from its centre. It is not known to Earthlings where this centre might lie. But the Earth is a child of its own Sun, one of the smaller stars. The Earth is in evolution *to align*, to return to its source, or Light vibration, as are all and everything. Mankind, womankind, their kind which are children, are a collectivity. One gain of altitude towards alignment - one inward surrender to grace - influences the whole. That is your ultimate wish to help others, until all are re-united in the ending of alienation and the sorrows that go with it.

"Life in the body, on Earth, is never static. It is like one great almond tree. All the buds eventually open. But some of them open quicker than others. Those that open earlier, may lead the rest. By this is meant rebirth or reincarnation. To incarnate is simply to take the carnal form; there are a myriad others, but those are outside the scope of our present work together. Those who take the carnal form on Earth, come back to it repeatedly until they can regain hold of the elixir they temporarily lost sight of. Now, this is something which you have seen clearly, or clairvoyantly, as they say down there. Knowledge of yourself came up the track and hit you broadside. It made you shudder. In other words, it *reverberated*, to use a Kabbalist term, and that manifests as repetition; as waves of sound and light to manifest. Shock replays itself until it becomes the consciousness that administered the shock, and is dispelled.

"Each lifetime is directed by a co-operation of its inner ruler with the fruit-bearing seeds of its former actions; but grace through prayer, attention and surrender can alter the determinant. This happens when the life force, espousing a new plane of being, perceives itself differently. It suffers its own self to learn, as 'the children to come unto Me'. The blind man contests his fate. The seer embraces it as his guide and providence. The mystery of suffering and alienation - called evil - is inscrutable to those on Earth.

"No body can judge his own birth, or that of another, as being good or bad, because no body is in a position to know the wheel's entirety, the realised Self of all these births, unless he or she is a great sage. The sage is one who judges not; only individuals judge themselves as they imagine. Do not worry about suffering. Be compassionate to the sufferer, but do not attempt to solve it. You eat the fruits of your karma. Everybody has to eat the fruit of his destiny to discover destination. This is the hardest of all lessons for those on Earth to learn. Many millions of souls are bathed in it. Their agony is in the regard, the silent song of the angel.

"Knowledge of other worlds will not help you just now. As an integral part of humankind, you are to return to Earth until you are earthed, until you awaken on the Tree of Humanity."

"Well, my guiding power," said Jeremy softly, "what are you going to do with me?"

"You will be born again into the same life. It will recur until you remember yourself at a dangerous corner. Then it will all be different."

After that, Jeremy knew no more.

* * *

As a speck of infinity, and as a chilled and blinkered babe, he was being born. He woke in his bed and cried, but could not remember what it was that he so burningly wanted. The hunger, the thirst of the walls around him, consumed him *and something else*. He shuddered.

As a dim spark among many stars, he voyaged through super-natural entities between them and was brought up short.

He found his mother and then his father, and lost consciousness. They drove into him with their ideas. But he became an accountant, for he was meticulous and stolid, and better at sums than they expected.

The womb was a place where he slept and grew and listened to his advisers until they dropped him. He knew it all before. He bellowed below. The moon waxed and waned, she was the right one for him, she stood fast in the land. He, a suspicious Virgoan, only read his stars in the papers, so he did not know that his powers of attraction and self-reflection were gathered in the Moon in Taurus for his fixed resettlement; a pattern, a habit. It was all in the mind, his train of thought. He knew it all before! He was terribly bored with the lesson. For some strange reason, his career at a minor public school (paid for by his uncle Arnold who was in the restaurant business), the games he was good at, his friends, his choice of figures, the skirts he lifted, the wife who annoyed him, the clients who reinforced him, all were *déjà vue*. And all of them somehow lost him. Like chewing gum, it had lost its flavour.

Two harbingers of a *secret* flavour, or drawer in his life were: his attractiveness to women, which he intensely enjoyed, and a curious casual ability to read peoples' palms and tell the future. This he had discovered quite by accident, it contributed to his success as a financial advisor, and made him on occasion wonder deeply about unexplainable things. As a little boy he wondered "why am I here again?" and kept on wondering. Every event, great or small in his life, was positioned in a place made ready for it; the expression surrounding him was "I told you so." At school, he loved the singing at morning assembly, particularly his favourite hymn "For Those in Peril on the Sea". He wished he could live dangerously, not knowing what would happen next, but did not know how. Over the years he developed an interesting and undemonstrative relationship with his aunt Mavis who, he had discovered, also had an undeclared fondness for Those in Peril on the Sea. She dressed eccentrically and kept up a running battle with his uncle Arnold in the restaurant business, who liked to keep up appearances; but she was a member of the Unitarian Church, and sometimes Jeremy liked to escort her to a service. Nobody else in his family was religious, so to do this was the mark of a rebel, and strangely enhanced the flavour of his *secret* life.

One day, Jeremy had a terrible dream that he was run over by a train, and it was entirely his own fault for not getting out of the way. He found himself emotionally shattered and plagued with remorse for the plight of the driver who for the rest of his life would have to live with what his train had done. The dream was far larger than life, and for a long time afterward, Jeremy could not *join himself up*. He heard of an eccentric philosopher in Ipswich who counselled persons who had lost their heads, but this seemed a little far fetched; having lost his feet also, he could not even walk. The inexplicable trauma was consigned to his secret life, but he sought help: a hypnotherapist with whom he pretended to go to sleep but in fact went to bed, and a behavioural technician who cost him a lot of good money.

Finally in despair he approached the Minister of aunt Mavis's Unitarian church. The Minister offered him a glass of good sherry, listened carefully to what he had to say, sat silent for a moment and then said, "This isn't a problem you or I or anyone can *solve*, Mr. Montfort. To live in *hope* of doing so, is falsehood. It is better to live without hope but *trusting* the way will be shown. If you hope by your limited effort to solve the problem of life, you build up its resistance against you. But if you live within the problem, *as the problem, with your awareness*, without trying to change it or have ideas about it, you may discover *an intimacy*, a relationship. This will reveal to you, most probably, the deeper power behind. There is a very interesting and distinguished Indian gentleman called J.Krishnamurti who speaks sometimes at Wimbledon. I don't agree with all he says, but one phrase of his has remained ever with me: *'Be the disciple of your understanding.'* The disciple, you know, is under the discipline of Higher Law."

Jeremy discovered a dual reaction in himself, to this advice. Part of him said "Gobbledygook". But he also left the vicarage deep in thought, and finding his problem *interesting*. There flashed in him for a moment, a sensation of his fear of trains not as a *disease*, but as *consciousness* ... just enough to intrigue his curiousity.

* * *

For many years, Jeremy's life was carefully constructed around his fear of trains and railways. Very occasionally he was able to get *into* the train itself and go on a journey like a child, looking through the windows of discovery. Mostly he accepted the shameful existence of his handicap as a bad job, and seldom left home. He kept in touch with the Unitarian Minister, and built up his career within these restrictions. His uncle Arnold having died at a ripe old age of food poisoning - from eating tinned pork while on holiday in Israel - he kept an eye also on his aunt Mavis, who was 'in the pink' as they say.

One day, an emergency arose. He received a letter from her by the morning's post, informing him that she would be arriving on the midday train from Sheffield at Kings Cross to go over with him, some discrepancies in her Will, her old eyes being not what they were. Would he be there to meet her, as she had never been able to find her way in the Big Smoke, and didn't intend to start now, at her time of life. Would he please wear that nice Paisley red necktie she gave him for his birthday, so she could see how it suits him, Ever your loving Auntie, with three kisses.

The unresolved problem of aunt Mavis's Will had been generating acrimony in the family, as the old girl kept capriciously changing her mind. Immediately after uncle Arnold's death she had had the telephone disconnected and taken away so as not to answer condolences; and so she had found it convenient to

73

remain - off limits to all interested parties, save her favourite nephew. Today, Jeremy hoped she might allow him to lodge the controversial document with his own solicitor.

His first impulse, at the prospect of an 'emergency' journey to Kings Cross station to meet aunt Mavis' train, was to reach for the Scotch. A strange counter-current stayed his arm. Occasionally there came to him these brief and curious episodes of a 'scientific' awareness of his trouble, of the pounding in his head and stomach. The pounding, the terror, continued, but he watched it. He couldn't say why. The bottom fell out of his world and another person ruled him. He felt as helpless as a psychopath. He called a taxi and went, clear headed, to meet his dangerous corner.

Carefully he made his way over the station concourse, trying to remember to breathe deeply, as the Minister had once advised him. His feet waded through deep sand, he walked on stumps. On the platform itself was gathered a large throng of people to meet the train. Jeremy stationed himself well back in the crowd and watched and heard, with horror and fascination the approach and sound of the dreadful engine of iron and wheels, the appalling hot cloud of smoke and screech of steam, grinding his stomach to molten metal as it slid inexorably towards buffer state. Never had he seen anything so frightful, so unspeakable. He looked and looked with awful perverse bravery, and almost wept. He perceived also in himself ... an unmentionable *attraction*.

Suddenly, Jeremy recalled, from forgotten years ago, that there is no need to meet aunt Mavis on the platform. In fact she would find him more easily if he retired to just behind the ticket barrier, through which the crowd of passengers and those to meet them must trickle, one by one. Let aunt Mavis come to meet *him*! This made a great deal of sense.

His head strangely clearing as he streamed rivers of sweat, Jeremy very carefully and deliberately retreated and stood his ground. He seemed to have no head at all now, but it didn't matter. With joyous equanimity the crowd passed through him like a flock of bright sheep and disappeared, and suddenly there was Auntie, bent and withered as an old apple, but quite steady on her pins and seizing his red Paisley tie with impish delight as she reached up to kiss him soundly on both cheeks ... and as beautiful as the proverbial maiden behind the dragon's tail. Jeremy was astonished at his state of mind, but handed over to it the reins of his obligation. With delicate gallantry he offered a strong arm to aunt Mavis, carried all her luggage with the other, glanced at the train which now sat, strangely small and dismembered like a pig in its platform trough, and took her to lunch at the Savoy.

"Dear boy," said aunt Mavis over coffee, mint biscuits and an excellent Armagnac - she enjoyed a bit of a tipple, it lit up the roses in her cheeks - "I am very happy with the way our business has gone. Yes dear, you take care of it all, I've got better things to think of now, before I pop off. On one condition." She seized his hand in her bony fingers and looked at him sharply. "All the nephews will get theirs, an equal share of Arnold's whack. But I want you to have yours now. Better you than the taxman, eh?"

"Oh Auntie, well, whatever you say of course, thanks most ..." said Jeremy inadequately, as Mavis produced from her green crocodile handbag a chequebook with a prancing black horse on it, in which she wrote in her firm clear hand. "There you are dear. Now you put that where the good apples grow, and we need say no more about it, heh?" Thumbing her nose roguishly, she handed it to him. They sat for a while in comfortable silence.

"Actually Auntie," said Jeremy "we do share a certain little secret. You know the Reverend Hornby?"

"Young Timothy? Yes of course."

"Well, he's been very kind and wise. Do you know what I want to do with your money?"

"Not my money, dear boy. Arnie's, and now your own. Go on."

"Well - I feel rather shy about this - I think I'll give up, you know, the accountancy practice and train for the Unitarian ministry. I feel very deeply about it. You didn't know that, did you? I want to be able to help people to ..."

"Oh good," said his aunt "How much better for you than all that nasty money grubbing. Let me know when I can hear your first sermon, and I'll make a Special Journey. Now dear, how about we jump on a nice red bus and take a tootle round the park?" She opened her suitcase (which she had refused to allow the waiter to remove) to show him. "Look dear. Three nice big loaves baked by Mr Sebastian Gubbins my baker specially, to feed the ducks."

"They won't go short," Jeremy agreed. "Auntie, do you know what the text of my first sermon will be? *Thy will be done.*"

And Jeremy Montfort awoke.

The Alchemist of Notre Dame
(from La Mystere des Cathedrales
Fulcanelli.)

In the Syllabus

IN THE early 21st century, the Ministry of Education placed "Entrepreneurship" on the syllabus for those over 16 who had chosen Business Studies. One of the major modules was "Damage Limitation" or How to Handle the Media if your Company is Embarrassed. Mr Burroughs, the senior lecturer in Media Studies at the Milton Freidman Business School, explained with difficulty to his students what was required. "Imagine," he said "that you are the chief executive of a multi-European conglomerate." He paused, rocked on his heels and continued: "Your company is suspected of endangering people's lives by a contaminated food product called EATME. This is a compound food cake, one slice of which provides you with a balanced diet. However - several cases of food poisoning have been traced to EATME. A TV news agency calls you. You agree to a meeting in your office, rather than antagonize the media. Now, the first step in Damage Limitation is to size up your interviewer. Remember the golden rule! you must protect the company …"

At that moment, the cell in Mr Burrough's trouser pocket bleeped. Three bleeps meant Go and see the Principal. "Excuse me, boys and girls," he said "I've got to go. Class, read my essay on Damage Limitation in the standard textbook you all have: *How to be an Entrepreneur, updated to 1999.* I will be back as soon as I can." Blenkinsop the assistant Principal, came into the classroom and hissed, "The old boy wants to see you right away in his office. I will take over the class from here. Good luck"

Burroughs put on his tie carefully, and then entered the Principal's office. Mr Sydney Grimm lived up to his name. "Look here Burroughs, we're in a fine mess. The media have discovered that your book is a plagiarized version of Professor Arthur

Hopkins' lectures last year to his students at Yale University. The Hopkins lectures were never published. You must have got hold of the notes. Now Burroughs, limit the damage damn you, for your sake, my sake and the sake of the school. Here are the TV boys, I'm off. Get us all out of it, Burroughs, or else."

Burroughs was in a state of mild shock. Quickly he rallied, knowing as he did that the first step in DL is *Don't Look Worried.* "Come in, great to see you, coffee?" he breezed, opening the door. There stood Sir David Questor, top interviewer at the Beeb, and presenter of the peak show *Inquisition.* "Hello, Sir David," he purred reverentially – (step Two, *be unctuous to the titled till you know their game.*) The great man peered at him through horny half framed library specs. "Right, Mr Antony Burroughs? I have some questions for tonight's programme about your very successful book. Are you ready for a live interview? Yes, come in, team."

Lights, camera crew and assistants poured into the office. Burroughs was trapped in the public eye. "Certainly," he said (step Three sprang to mind: *Stall*) – "providing you do not edit what I say until I have seen it." "Of course I agree," replied Sir David. "We will talk live for five minutes – no need for make-up or any editing. OK team, let's go!"

Sir David settled himself with a flourish at the Principal's desk, blandly regarded his scurrying minions, and introduced him. "Well, tonight I am speaking to Mr Antony Burroughs, senior lecturer in Entrepreneurship at the Milton Freidman Business School, author of the educational best-seller *How to Be an Entrepreneur 2000.* Tell me, Antony, when did you read Professor Arthur Hopkins lecture series he gave to his students at Yale? The *Daily Investigator* has discovered that your book and those unpublished lectures are virtually identical."

Burroughs smiled pleasantly, masking his fear, *how did they sniff that out?* "Could you repeat the question?" (step Four, *play for time, he only has five minutes*). He added for emphasis "I did not follow your innuendo." (step Five, *when in dead trouble, the best defense is attack.*)

Sir David repeated, "Have you read the Hopkins lectures, they are the same as your book."

"Which Hopkins do you mean?"

"Hopkins of Yale, naturally."

"Oh yes, yes, Hopkins of Yale, a grand fellow. Yes. Remarkable man. Great pedagogue. Funny you should mention him, I recall seeing him at the Pan-European Conference in 1997. Great man isn't he, most eloquent, brilliant, he told me then that ..." Sir David cut him in midstream – "Please answer the question." Burroughs tried to remember step Six. "Now look here, Sir David!" All of a sudden, the bleeps went off in his trouser pocket.

Sweat on his brow, Burroughs woke and groped for his bedside alarm. It was still dark. It was only a nightmare, thank God. "I'll tell the little blighters at college my dream, and set them the problem. No, better not – they aren't fools ... I think I'll give Hopkins a call." Straight away he dialed out to Connecticut. "Hello Arthur? Antony here, havn't gone to bed yet have you? how are you, good good good, fine fine. Fine. Never better. Not too late to call, I hope? Oh good. Excellent. And how is Marji? I'm very, very glad to hear it. Good. Yes. Yes. Hahahah, you don't say. Must be going down the tubes. Dreadful. Dreadful. Oh well, I'm absolutely delighted. Delighted. Well Arthur, I just wanted to remind you that if any one finds out our, you know, arrangement, deny it, and I'll continue to give you 80 per cent of the royalties, else we'll both be for the high jump won't we."

"Yeah, sure, sure. Sure thing. I was gonna call you myself. Y'know, I had this real crazy dream, yeah?"

"No! so did I … you mean that someone found out … ?"

"Yeah, well that's kinda spooky. Anyway, forewarned is forearmed, Marji's doing just fine, so enjoy your day, cheer-bye."

***

A week later, after he had almost forgotten the matter, Antony received in his trouser pocket, another summons to Grimm's office.

"You will be pleased to hear, Antony," said his superior, morosely bowling a pill along the desk before dropping it in his tumbler of water "that some media boy's been saying your stuff was written just like Hopkins, and what did I think? So I called Hopkins myself and checked."

"Great man. Great man. Great. Great."

"He strongly denied any connection. Said he'd read your book and it is highly original. These were the exact words he used. In fact he also said he based some of his unpublished lectures on it."

"Oh well. Most kind of you … "

"Yes," said Grimm. "Now Antony, be a real good entrepreneur and give me twenty per cent of your royalties for getting you out of the shit. This is a school for entrepreneurs, and any little cash-flow problem could be embarrassing, wouldn't it? After all, we're in the education business – good value for money and all that. Practise what we *preach*, agreed? or I may be looking to replace you." The pill fizzed, and Grimm drank and pulled a face.

If there was a Hippocratic Olympics, thought Antony bitterly, the old fart would win the gold medal. "Yes Sydney of course, no problem. No problem. None at all. We must all be enterprising and limit each other's damage, after all's said and done, it's in the higher educational syllabus, this glorious year of our Lord, A-men."

"Yes, so glad you understand," said Grimm. "Oh, and that reminds me. I must go and take school prayers. It's compulsory now, and in the syllabus since last year. For your own good and our good, Antony, you had better come with me."

The Thought Machine

AT LONG last, science made the greatest breakthrough since the invention of the phone! It was called "The Thought Machine". It would be revealed to the astonished world to celebrate the Millennium.

Briefly, our scientists have already for some years, been able to measure their brain activity online. As they sit face to screen, they observe with rapture the mountain range of their credible, cerebral ponderings. A new software can now analyse those peaks, waves and trembling coloratura into coherent patterns of thought. A further sophistication translates the elaborate celestial geometries by reduction, into individual words. Yet another reduction, and the thinker's language is impulsed at will to "record". When strapped firmly around the forehead, his thoughts are revealed on screen, for real, for all to see.

This closely guarded development would be unleashed on an unsuspecting but worshipful public, to open the second Millennium. Its enamoured creators agreed among themselves that the potential was enormous. If the brain can dazzle – let there be the speed of light.

Professor Hyman Chomsky of Moscow and Professor Fairbanks Zimmermann Jun. of Harvard, were willing guinea pigs. They and their teams worked closely together for years online, but have not physically met. Over the Millennium, relations between the two erstwhile superpowers are so good, having taken their knocks from the rest of the world, that their virtual cooperation is speedy and harmonious. Should the new invention go first to governments, to decide on its application? The Professors browsed happily on their individual screens. The police would find it invaluable! So will the intelligence services, spy cameras, school teachers, customs & excise, young lovers, and every relationship where "an understanding" is essential. What a boon to lawyers, psychiatrists and their clients, and particularly to those from whom, in doctors' surgeries, delicate information is with-held! Local government and tax inspectors will benefit. It will cut red tape in the affairs of family and business, and save the Economy. What a godsend!

So helpful is this software to all who wish to sat-nav the thoughts of others, that the buzz-word *Truth Machine* generates an ecstatic graph of good will among high-echelon cranial screens. The device should be issued to each world citizen like a gas mask in wartime.

The great day dawned, for the final testing.

Professor Chomsky and Professor Fairbanks Zimmermann Jun. both flew to London to meet on neutral terrain. They greeted each other with a round of warm Soviet kisses and Yankee slaps on the back, and sat down. In the hush that greets the making of history, each put on his screen.

On Chomsky's screen there flashed at once: "Silly old fat pompous buffer. Pretentious fart with a name like that. Bound to steal all the best ideas. I'll put a stop to that." Zimmermann's screen flashed an instant reciprocation: "Well, of all the rotten wetmouth so-and-sos. Calls himself a Chomsky – sure has diabolic low cunning. And he smells. SO THAT'S WHAT HE THINKS.'

Both men blushed with shame, looked at each other and realized they are unable to control the truth - their instant reactions.

After hastily removing their screens and sinking a great deal of vodka, some repairs were shakily re-established. The two men decided that for the general good, the Thought Machine should not be used at all. Nobly they agreed to delete every vestige of their collaborative work, rather than risk the sole privacy left to man, that of his very intimate thoughts. Heartily they shook hands. Zimmermann said, relieved at being able again to rely on communication two or three stages removed from chaos, "You know Chomsky, my old pal, sometimes discretion is the better part of valour." Chomsky warmly agreed, with more kisses: "Yes comrade, we will work together. We will work on something else that is not the thought reading. Let's develop some software for the Synthesizing Intelligence instead. We both need it."

And so History continued.

The Unknown Factor

MANY YEARS ago, I got a tap on the shoulder – one of many to come – which woke me. As with many conscripts to National Service, the period 1949-51 was for me a time of difficult adjustment. Most of the Army had demobilized, leaving a hard core of regulars. These heroes of El Alamein, Burma and the liberation of Europe, were suddenly faced with raw schoolboys to train as soldiers. It was an arduous bridge for both sides to cross. One man who achieved the crossing for me, was a certain Captain Carter.

Carter was the epitome of rough-diamond military bearing. He had a look of Errol Flynn, down to the exact detail of the moustache. One of his favourite training methods was to order the squad to the local wood, and drill us to "walk like cats". We had to feel our way as if by night, with full attention and without a sound, under his incessant fire. The poor pimpled lads tried like moon walkers, to copy a cat. They snapped fallen branches and lurched awkwardly under their kit, as their rifles tangled with the twigs. "I said a CAT, a CAT you dam' fool! not a sex starved rhino. You ever seen a cat before? I said a hundred times and I'll say it again, the ENEMY SURROUNDS US. DON'T GET CAUGHT OUT. WATCH!"

Back in barracks after the "enemy awareness exercises", Carter lectured us on a subject called TEWTS, or what was officially called Tactical Exercises Without Troops. In the Nissen hut, there was a model of a battle terrain. He harangued us for over half an hour: *"the success of any battle is ninety-nine percent due to making certain that each and every detail is planned so carefully that you can neither fail nor be surprised. Only one thing can defeat you. THE UNKNOWN FACTOR."*

Captain Carter had a bee in his bonnet about this. If he said it once, he said it a hundred times: it was in all his other drillings as well. All military planning must ensure it is NEVER caught out by this unknown factor. In my barracks the factor itself became known as the Un-mown Carter.

Having exhaustively covered every small ramification of strategy and tactics in his imaginary battle plan, one day he asked *Were there any questions*? No one moved. We were all a little afraid of his ferocity.

He asked again. Still no questions. "Right," said he, "no one leaves this class room till a question is asked."

Total, ringing, creeping silence."

"Right. You're all lily white. Now I'm going to ask YOU a question. See if you heard a word I said. Which of you boys can tell me which is THE MOST IMPORTANT FACTOR in a battle?" For due emphasis he wrote it on the board, stood back and bristled.

Not a word. A long pause. The buzzing of bluebottles. Ears being awkwardly scratched, pencils chewed, desks stabbed, bladders squirm. He would keep us here all night.

Timidly, I raised my hand.

"WELL?"

"Sir," I replied, "the most important factor in any battle is the unknown one."

"UNKNOWN FACTOR!" he roared, beside himself "Where the

hell did you get that totally ridiculous idea from. Absolute piffle. There is no such thing as an unknown factor. Poppycock. If I've said it once, I've said it a hundred times, the success of any battle is due to meticulous and exact planning, every detail, no more or less. There's no such thing as surprises. Unknown factor. Absolute rubbish. Who ever heard of ..."

For a long time I was lambasted with this tirade. Finally he sneeringly dismissed the class. As I left, tail between my legs, he came up to me, put his hand on my shoulder and whispered in my ear "Do you know what that was, Jacobs?"

"No Sir," I replied meekly, rather dazed.

"That was the Unknown Factor!"

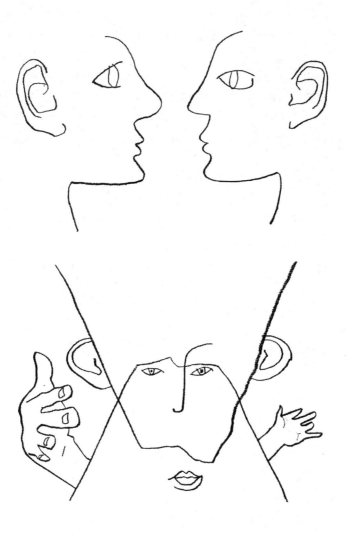

The Uncles - Another Cautionary Tale

From a Story by Laura Jacobs

CUTHBERT AND Roger were twins. They were five years old, looked exactly alike, and had no brothers or sisters. So they were very good friends indeed, because it was just like looking in the mirror. Nobody could tall them apart except Mummy and Daddy. Their names were chosen after their two Uncles, Daddy's brother Cuthbert who got lost in America, and Mummy's brother Roger who stayed at home and got a big job printing books and making lots of money.

Roger and Cuthbert agreed in their own private language, that they should know more about these two Uncles with their names, who were so different. So they decided to ask Mummy and Daddy.

Mummy replied that she would tell them all about their Uncles. But it was a very long, long story, so every evening she would tell them just a little more, so that they would understand. Daddy sat as usual in his chair in front of the fire, and smoked his pipe.

"Well," said Mummy, "when your Uncle Cuthbert was little, just about your age, he had everything he ever wanted. His Daddy gave him lots of pocket money so he could buy sweets and ice-cream as often as he wanted. Wherever he wanted to go, he was taken, to football matches, to the zoo, and to every so many films. He had a shiny bicycle and used to ride around the garden to his heart's content and then come in for lunch and tea – which was all ready for him – without being asked to do anything. Not even the washing up.

"When your Uncle Roger was little, his Daddy was very strict and he only had a little pocket money, not enough to buy very much, so he saved in his piggy bank. If he wanted more, he had to do odd jobs like helping his Mummy clean the house and tidy the kitchen, or help Daddy in the garden. Sometimes he washed the car.

"Uncle Cuthbert always got his own way, and if he did not get it immediately, he would scream and kick until he was allowed to do what he wanted."

Roger and Cuthbert looked in the mirror by the fireplace and burst out laughing. "What about Uncle Roger?" said Cuthbert.

"Oh, Uncle Roger could scream and kick until he was blue in the face, but he just got left alone, until one day he said to himself that this was no good. And he went and asked instead, what would Mummy and Daddy like him to do?"

The little boys laughed so hard at this, that they swallowed down the wrong way, and had to be banged on the back.

"Now," said Mummy "First I shall tell you a Cuthbert story, and then next time, a Roger story." "Can we start tonight? Please?" said the boys. "No," said Mummy. "It is too late. We will leave it till tomorrow. Now go and brush your teeth and say goodnight." So Roger and Cuthbert romped with their Daddy and tried to pull him off his chair. Then they brushed their teeth, looked in the mirror, said goodnight and soon were fast asleep.

***

Next day after supper, Mummy began. "I'm going to tell you about your Uncle Cuthbert at the zoo," she said. "One day, little

Cuthbert said he wanted to go to the zoo. 'If I don't,' he said 'I will scream.' 'Alright,' said his Daddy, and asked Phillips the chauffeur to put on his uniform, get the car out, give it a clean, and take him. Uncle Cuthbert sat in the back of the big car, while Phillips drove from their house near the Park, to the zoo. 'Come on,' said Phillips, 'in we go.' 'Can I have an ice-cream,' said Uncle Cuthbert. 'Of course you can,' said Phillips, and bought him a very large one. The sun was very hot, so some of it melted. Cuthbert had a lovely day looking at the animals, especially the monkeys. They had funny faces, and they hung upside down and chattered, and didn't wipe their bottoms. 'I want to feed a monkey,' said Uncle Cuthbert. 'Alright,' said Phillips, and bought a large bag of cashew nuts for him. Uncle Cuthbert put his hand right into the cage with some nuts. The monkey grabbed at it, and before you could say Jack Robinson, bit his arm very hard. Cuthbert began to cry, and said 'I want to go home.' 'Alright,' said Phillips 'but remember it is very dangerous to feed monkeys without being careful.'"

The little boys laughed and laughed at this, especially at the bit where Uncle Cuthbert got bitten. "Did he get Septisseemia?" they said. "No he didn't," replied Mummy "but it was very sore for several days." "Now tell us a Roger story!" they said, jumping about. "Alright," said Mummy, "tomorrow I will tell you about Uncle Roger and his visit to the zoo. Now it's time for bed. " Daddy agreed to be an elephant at the zoo, and they rode on his back all the way upstairs to the bathroom, had a bath, looked in the mirror and said goodnight; then they jumped into bed with their biggest Old Teddy, and soon were fast asleep.

***

When they woke up, the boys couldn't wait to hear what had happened to Uncle Roger at the zoo. They tried to get Mummy to tell them at breakfast, but she wouldn't. All day, even at school, they wondered how he got on.

At last in the evening, Daddy chopped some wood, lit the fire, puffed on his pipe and knocked out the dottle, and Mummy was ready to continue the story. "Sit down, boys," she told them. "Now, one day your Uncle Roger asked his Daddy if he could go to the zoo. 'Yes,' said his Daddy 'if you have enough money in your piggy bank. Tell you what. You take 50 pence out of Piggy, and I will pay the rest.' Roger had saved up two pounds, so he thought it would be alright. 'Good,' said Daddy 'We will walk, shall we? It's only a mile away. Come on, we won't need our coats.'

When they got to the zoo, Uncle Roger was amazed. There was so much to see. He looked carefully at every animal. He looked at the big growly lion with its red mane, it dozed on a rock just like an enormous cat. And he looked at the huge elephant with its flappy ears and wrinkly feet for such a long time, that the elephant came up and took an apple from him, with its trunk. Uncle Roger was thrilled. He also enjoyed the funny monkeys and the beautiful coloured birds. Some of them sang so loudly, he had to put his hands over his ears. He saw the camel, looking hot and cross, and the giraffe with its long neck and pretty eyelashes. He saw a very strange ostrich with its head in the sand; but when it came up and looked at him, it looked rather like a giraffe, it had lovely eyes and fur all down its neck changing into feathers. His Daddy explained that ostriches cannot fly because their feathers are not strong enough for their big bodies, and that they come from South Africa on the other half of the world. Then they saw a kangaroo with her baby in her pocket, and some very smelly goats. One of them came up and tried to eat Uncle Roger's shirt. They visited the Insect House, and Uncle Roger watched the ants building a little bridge to cross the stream. Next they went to the

Snake House, and Uncle Roger saw a boa constrictor fast asleep, and a very poisonous black mamba hissed at him. On their way out they stopped to see the sea lions being fed, which was splashy and exciting, and said hello to a rhinoceros. The rhinoceros didn't reply, and looked scratchy and bad tempered. Uncle Roger's Daddy explained that this is because he has fruitcake crumbs under his skin, and told him he would read him a Just So Story when they got home, and then tell him about real rhinoceroses. 'Well now,' said his Dad 'you have studied so hard, I'm going to buy you an ice-cream, but don't think I'll do this every time. What flavour would you like? Let's walk home now, and you tell Mummy all about it.' '

The boys smiled, and looked in the mirror.

Daddy wanted to play the gramophone, so they went straight up to bed, and Cuthbert looked at Roger, and Roger looked at Cuthbert, and smiled again. Then they got under the covers and asked Mummy to play 'Where's my Boy'. Soon they were fast asleep.

At breakfast, Roger asked Mummy "what flavour ice-cream did Uncle Roger's Daddy get him?" "Your favourite," said Mummy, and rattled the plates in the sink. She didn't like washing up, and looked forward to the time when the boys would be old enough to do it. "Strawberry and chocolate."

"I wish I could have an ice-cream now," said Cuthbert "'stead of having to go to school. I don't want to go to school." This evening," said Mummy "I'm going to tell you about Uncle Cuthbert and Uncle Roger's first days at school. So be good boys now."

All day long, they could hardly wait.

After supper, Mummy lit the fire, because she and Daddy had had an argument – she thought he smoked his pipe too much – and he had gone out for a walk.

"Uncle Cuthbert," she said "did not like school. He wanted to stay at home and watch television. It was much more fun. But he had to go, so Phillips put on his uniform, got out the big car, gave it a rub, and took him to Basinghall Lodge where, at five years old he was to start. When your Uncle Cuthbert found out that he would wear a pink and blue cap and blazer, he thought this was rather fun. So he didn't kick and scream.

"At Basinghall Lodge, there were lots of other little boys Cuthbert's age, but no girls. On this first day, they all ran around the playground in two teams, the Pinks and the Blues. The game was to push the Pinks to the other side of a white line in the middle of the playground, and for the Pinks to push the Blues. Cuthbert was chosen to be a Pink. He liked pushing the Blue boys. "Well done Cuthbert!" someone called. It was his Mummy watching to see if he was alright. At that moment Cuthbert was so excited he fell down and banged his knee. Matron had to put on iodine and a sticking plaster. This hurt, so Uncle Cuthbert cried. That was his first day.

"Uncle Roger's first day at school was quite different. He walked with his Dad to the local primary school where there were girls and boys. The first game was a tug of war. The boys had one end of the rope with a red hanky tied round the middle, and the girls were on the other. Uncle Roger pulled very, very hard, but the girls were strong too, and it ended in a draw. Roger did not mind, he enjoyed the pulling.

"Uncle Cuthbert never liked school. He was fidgety and didn't hear most of what Mr Fawdrey the teacher said. He saw other boys making little round balls of paper, dipping them in the inkwell and then flicking them, when Mr Fawdry was writing on the blackboard. So he did it too, but Mr Fawdry turned round and saw him, and he was sent home. His Mummy told him he would have to try harder, but then she got the cook to make him his favourite treacle sponge cake to cheer him up.

"Uncle Roger was very interested in what his teacher said, and listened carefully. His book of writing, reading and adding up numbers was quite often marked with an A, which meant Very Good. But sometimes he got Bs and Cs too, which are not so good. He was not allowed to watch TV unless his Dad said the programmes would help with his school work. But he liked to learn about animals and birds, so he was allowed to stay up late sometimes to watch programmes about wild-life.

"And so the boys went on as they began. Uncle Cuthbert had to be taken away from Basinghall Lodge and have a tutor, Mr Parsons, who gave him lessons at home. Uncle Roger stayed at school and did his homework, so he is now an artist and draws those beautiful pictures of nature and wild animals in books. Now it's time for bed!"

Daddy had come in from his walk, but was rather grumpy. "You do as your Mother says," he said, when the twins tried to tickle him, and started to light his pipe again.

Upstairs, Cuthbert went right up to the mirror and kissed it. Roger did exactly the same. "Why did Uncle Cuthbert get lost in 'Merica?" they asked their Mummy when she came upstairs. "Because he grew up a very handsome man, and he decided to be a film star," she said, tucking them up and making quite sure – as she often did – that they had not left their feet behind in the bathroom. The twins made it very difficult for her, because they kept hiding them under the pillow. This was one of their favourite games.

"Uncle Cuthbert had such a handsome face and enjoyed looking at his reflection in the mirror so much that one day he fell right into it, and got lost. He was very spoiled when he was a little boy, so he hadn't learnt to find his own way. Phillips always drove him everywhere in the big car, and his Mummy and Daddy always gave him what he wanted. But everyone has to fall into the looking glass when they grow up, to find out for themselves. It's very easy to get lost in America, especially if you want to be on television. It's an enormous country and full of pretty faces already. Of course there are lots of other, really wonderful things to find there too, Daddy and I will tell you all about America another time. This little piggy went to market, this little piggy stayed at home. This piggy had roast beef, but this piggy had none. And this poor teeny little pink piggy got lost and cried wee wee weeeee, all the way home. Now go to sleep scallywag, good night."

***

That night, the little boys had a dream.

Uncle Roger set out in a canoe, just like the ones in the Park, to paddle across the Attalantic-ocean to America. He was going to look for Uncle Cuthbert. He took with him the prettiest book he had made, full of coloured pictures of lions, leopards and birds in Africa. At the same moment, Uncle Cuthbert, who was tired of being lost, set out in a canoe just like the ones in the Park, to paddle across the Attalantic-ocean to England. He had decided to come home. He took with him just one looking glass, with his prettiest face in it.

In the middle of the Attalantic Ocean, at a very hard, bright misty place called Atlantis, the two Uncles met, and could paddle no further, however hard they tried. Uncle Roger paddled and paddled. Uncle Cuthbert did exactly the same.

Finally they gave up, and stayed quite still. Uncle Cuthbert saw the far horizon, the great blue sea and white sky. So did Uncle Roger. In this place, both Uncles looked through each other into the wide world all around. "Attaboy," said Uncle Roger. "Atman," said Uncle Cuthbert. Then Uncle Cuthbert held up the mirror with his pretty face in it, and Uncle Roger held up the book with his pictures of wild life in Africa, and the sun shone.

They were very happy in Atlantis, and Mummy and Daddy got married. Sometimes it got a little foggy. All they had to do was polish the fog with a finger, and it became bright and clear again.

***

"Mummy," said Roger the next morning at breakfast "Uncle Cuthbert came home."

"Yes darling, I know he did," said his Mummy, and gave him a kiss. "Now it's time for school. Have you got your pencil case?"

Space for the World to Happen in

Redundant yet again!

Liquidation wipes even skilled PC engineers off the map. It took months and months to get this job. He's sick of the ceaseless round of applications and interviews.

"Why not do something useful for *yourself*, for a change?" said his friend Tom that evening, over a beer. "You know – find out where you're really at Home. Make that your priority. Might even help you get a job that sticks. You're just out to lunch all the time, you aren't concentrating, you know that."

Fred didn't. Tom had a habit of throwing out enigmatic aphorisms, which made people want to hit him sometimes, but he was an annoyingly good drinking companion. Tom's life-style seemed uncluttered, he had time for everybody, and for the crest of the wave, and always spoke his mind. Perhaps he's got a new age guru …? Fred teased him for a while.

"No, I don't bother with all that," said Tom "but I do know someone who's written a few books. I read one years ago, which turned my whole *attitude* upside down, he became a friend." "You mean, you got a shrink? Someone with all the *smart answers*?" "Nah. Just a friend who stays with the question. You might say he's on the ball, you might not." "Your round, then," said Fred, irritated and intrigued. But an hour later, he'd written down a phone number: something to do for himself, ditch the Jobseekers, take a day out in East Anglia for a change …

The voice on the line next morning was deep, fruity and rather inviting. "My name is Douglas. I live near Ipswich. Get the 11.10

103

from Liverpool Street next Saturday, and we'll meet you at the station." Fred stalled: "Hey, you don't know me." "You're a friend of Tom's. Any good friend of his ..." "Well, thanks. That's really kind, if you're sure. See you on Saturday." There was a dulcet rumble in Fred's ear: "You can stay for the weekend if you like, there's no one in the spare room at the moment. I have a beard, and I'll be in a mini-minor."

This sounded terrifying. But Saturday duly came, and Fred's cold feet weren't taking him anywhere. "I'm not trekking out there to see this crazy old geezer with his beard and his tin heap," he told Tom. "So what will you do instead?" said Tom. "Go on – just be an explorer. What have you got to lose? He's my friend. Don't you trust me?"

The train arrived at Ipswich nine minutes late: the passengers chattered urgently to their mobiles, back to back. But in the car-park, by the open door of his mini, stood a sturdy, avuncular personage with piercing eyes, neatly dressed in a tweed jacket. "Hello, you must be Fred. Well, how nice to meet you Fred, I'm Douglas Harding. So you've come to see what peculiar looking people we are? And the recession's hit you too? Awful the way we need the infrastructure. Hop in."

After a series of ribbons and roundabouts, they turned off into an oak-lined lane. An unexpected rural landscape welled up and slowed the clock. The glaringly metalled business parks and by-pass routes seemed a dust of by-gone dreams. The small car cramped Fred's long legs, and rattled along, close to the ground. As dappled bands of sunlight and silage flowed through him, making him blink, Fred's suspicion began to relax. "What's this, a time machine?" he asked. "You know, I grew up in a place like this. You'd never believe the country being so close to the town." "So it is," said his host. He used his voice, deep and unhurried, as an actor does, thoroughly enjoying its flavour. "I'm a local boy myself. Lowestoft. Then I became an architect. You'll see, I built my own house, it was rather avant-garde then, back in the Fifties. Here we are."

They had driven into the annexe of a long low bungalow, hidden by a wall grown over with clematis. There were glimpses of a large green lawn, a pair of pheasants enjoying the sunshine, a bluebell wood, some stacks of chopped firewood, and – through a window in the trees - a shy stone church tower on a hill. Inside seemed to be a very large room, one wall almost entirely of glass. "Come onto the patio outside. Tea or coffee?"

Fred leaned back, enjoyed the warmth and launched into his problem, believing by now that the old man being a successful architect, could give him some practical advice, or even a recommendation. But Douglas quietly gazed at a glory of spring daffodils, and said it's all quite simple. (Who the hell is he kidding?) "Everyone," Douglas went on, as if he hadn't heard a word Fred said, "takes years and years of long search, libraries and libraries of reading, and ruinously expensive trips to the Orient to consult sages in out-of-the-way places. But let's get straight to the point. This I'm going to give you is, believe it or not, not the Long Search, but the Quick Find. Who are you *really*?" He curled his hand swiftly up and pointed straight at his own face. "Come on, Fred. You do the same. Now, what are you pointing at?"

"Me. My face of course. But this is – "

"Your face? No. Be honest. What do you actually *see*? That's right, go on pointing at it. Go on looking … at nothing, pronounced No Thing. Keep looking."

This actually startled Fred.

"Now sit back" – a theatrical gesture of bedside-manner – "really comfortably. That's it. Now what are you looking *out of*, at what you are pointing *to*?"

"My eyes of course," said Fred, good-naturedly copying his host's little game, but embarassed.

"No." A chuckle, basso profundo. "Be honest – on present evidence alone, and not what you've been told to believe. Be honest, and *concentrate*. Take your time. Is that really what you see? ... Aren't you actually an open window with no frame? Keep looking!"

With baffled instinct, Fred concurred. What was there to see? How boring. Nothing. The tip of a finger pointing, like that of Lord Kitchener, imperiously, accusatively, into him: and blurred with double vision, anger, and his nose in the way. Your country needs you. Your country needs you to fight and get killed. Your country needs to make you redundant. It is shocking. Through this unavoidability, a greenish blur of trees, grass and cheeping birds, the square church tower and the enquiring face of Douglas, also earnestly looking at him. This is uncomfortable and makes Fred blush, but like a rabbit on the road, he cannot move. And thus they remained for a while.

Then Douglas began mellifluously, to fill in some details. "Now you've got the point. We'll go into it slowly and scientifically. You believe you have a face, your very own, it's you. It gets you a job, it gets you a girlfriend, you feed it, it's your fortune and your misery, you shave it every morning, and sometimes after tea. Ever since you were little, they pointed at it and said 'That's Fred! He did it." Now, how does that make you feel?

"Have you ever actually seen this thing, without a mirror? Is that thing over there in the mirror Fred? Here – take a look. And go on seeing what you really see, here and now ..." (the finger point, again.) "Does that thing in the mirror fit YOU? does it fit on your shoulders – go on, measure it! Try it on! Isn't it the WRONG WAY ROUND? Didn't it get Narcissus into a pack of trouble?

"I can't see my face any other way" (still pointing) – "can you? So we have the immensity in common. This is our *friendship*. Along with the billions of human beings, and all life on this planet, flowers, ants, elephants. We are all *seers*. We are all looking from and into HERE, the window with no frame. Isn't that ASTON-ISHING?"

"But I can feel my face," said Fred.

"Ah yes, I do too – it's warm, it's bony here and very wrinkled there, it tickles, it's feelie-touchy, I'm always checking on it ... but doesn't my real, ineffable, immaculate and original face INCLUDE all that?" Douglas grimaced. "So Fred, am I just a potato, peeping through two little holes? Am I a sort of meatball? Is *this – all this* ..." (he waved his arm around the garden and the sunny poplar trees) "wet, dark, sticky inside?"

"Now," the old man went on remorselessly, and quite uncon-cerned whether this was relevant to Fred's unemployment or not, "now that we've got this far, WHERE IS MY FACE, THEN? WHERE'S YOURS? What can we put here instead?" – pause. "Why! " he went on, spreading his arms wide again, to include garden, house, church, pheasants, molehills and Fred himself. "Do I have any choice? Isn't THIS my real face? Isn't all this my face, and doesn't it fit perfectly HERE?" (tracing a swift arc across his upper chest). "And doesn't yours? this garden we enjoy together today -when you are in London, and I get up in the morning here at Shollond, and it all moves on - aren't I, aren't you, *space for the world to happen in?*"

Fred remained bemused. He clutched at vanity, bored and blank.

"You see now," said Douglas, pointing first to himself and then to Fred, "we trade faces. I have your face *here*, for which I thank you, you are much better looking than old Douglas. You have my face, as far as I'm concerned, over there, where I'm quite comfortable with it, thank you very much. I am eternally young here, the room for Fred to happen in. You are room for old Douglas to happen in. Now look down, and take your time about it. What do you see? Yes, point to it – the horizon, the cows, the field fence, and keep coming closer, the ground, the grass is getting rather long, yes, and here are our own feet, trousers, yes, a shirt, and we're both wearing ties today … in that order. Keep pointing … And then what? Are those legs and feet, is the headless torso in your view, perceived in any way *apart* from the grass, the field and trees, the sky on this glorious day, the galaxies of outer space we read about, the stars, the ATOMS? Where does it ever end?

"All *that* … is only the second object in my world. Closer than my breath as the mystics say, is the first – the intimate *mysterium*. Everything, the entire universe, connects to it. Space for the world to happen in, is where *"mine Eye is single, and my body filled with light'*, do you know that wonderful quotation from the gospel of Thomas? – Yes, for the world to happen in, and I mean ALL of it - the electric saw over the road, the blackbird's song, those lovely daffodils, my tummy rumbling – sorry! – and the political mess, the lost jobs, the great philosophers and saints, the sun's warmth, the pain, the worries – the whole universe, since before the big bang until beyond the stars, begins this unique space where my shoulders and my chest fade out."

Fred felt dizzy. But everyone has their face. It's common sense, isn't it.

"Nothing so uncommon as the common sense," quoted Douglas "as Bertrand Russell used to say. The problem dear boy, is out there where the mirror is. The problem is not in here at all. When you were little, did you know you had a face? And when you looked in the mirror and agreed with them that there it is, weren't you indoctrinated, converted to a belief? And didn't you forget all about this original one here, and didn't it get dull? And aren't we trying still, to figure it all out with our HEADS? – and don't we draw a blank? *What heads?* Can you see one? I can't. Didn't I tell you? - we are rather peculiar looking people, here.

"Now, that thing has its uses. People recognize you by the front of your brain – did that ever occur to you? And it finds you work, and gets you in trouble, and so on. It's very useful indeed – a godsend. But if we are really, really truthful with ourselves, *on present evidence alone,* the feast is on the table HERE, all the time, every instant. Where's that delicious sandwich going? – those flowers – that aeroplane – ha ha! – my right leg hurts – and that job you're looking for! It will come at the right time, because you will be receptive for it. Relax, Fred. Try living like this for a start. All it takes, is concentration. It will increase, and you'll experience more, but it takes *practice.*"

***

The two pheasants sidled over the lawn to take crumbs and grain from the old man's hands. Each visitor is for him an opportunity to trade faces, examine the evidence and refresh *the point*, all over again. The old man is not in fact a teacher, as commonly under-stood. He *shares the voyage.* He knows well that he knows nothing; that left to himself without *the practice* with every single visitor and friend, *the seeing* would atrophy. Sceptics sense this, and respond to the process, to try it out for themselves.

Later on, Douglas and Fred went for a stroll to the Orwell estuary. The vision was too unsettling for Fred to take in, but a certain down-to-earth innocence appealed to him, and he began to experiment cautiously. In front, the pathway through the woods to the shining water, flowed into his wide angle. Behind him space, undimensioned and unburdened, accommodated it all. He played a game as he walked, as the trees, the brook, houses and cars along the road – and even Douglas - entered himself and ... disappeared. He began to let go, and received a depth of field. And he realized that through conditioning he had forgotten how to see, and was therefore 'out of a job', and that *to see* is a creative exertion. The moment rejoices in the warm smell of cows. In brief flashes of rekindled colour, the world is a banquet of the child's surprise. In those brief flashes, the space flowing through houses and hedgerows is a song for the lover.

Glancing at Douglas, Fred wondered if he "had it" all the time. As if reading his thought, Douglas rejoined that the "natural state" has to be constantly and devotedly recalled; the essence of the Divine is this. An image came to Fred, of clearing a floor for a dancer. "It is called," said Douglas richly "living without a head, Fred. Look here!" – he swung his forefinger to a PASSING PLACE sign in the narrow lane – "Even Nacton district council helps me to see."

The new way of being the world as its seer, unstressed and imperturbably deep, promised to accommodate acute joy and pleasure, as also sorrow, striving and disappointment. He, Fred, was the nearest object in his sight: an actor in the never ending story. A profound and childlike curiosity began to touch him here and there; as if the tension of his *inattention* fell away. Back in

London, his brand new welcome mat would await the real adventure coming into his space. In fact, the adventure was here and now. He saw both ways. He watched, as Douglas with a private wrist movement discreet and fluid, pointed to himself and outward, like a bird's inseparable wings.

When they got back to the house, there was a visitor – but she was trimming the stalks of broccoli to make a quiche for supper, so she was obviously very much at home. Douglas introduced the exuberant but delicately built Frenchwoman in her sixties as "my friend Catherine", and looked at and embraced her with a tenderness which spoke a great deal more. More than anything Douglas had said, Fred was touched by the unusual sight of two old people in love, and 'built open' for each other. This world's wonderment glowed. Wasn't it perhaps his luck, to be expelled from the rat-race.? Where values are rightly placed, the means tend to be supplied by a different kind of management, to live, and not merely survive.

***

"Yes," said Tom, after Fred's return. "You've seen the point. Live that way, and everything will be different. Doesn't it give more sense of freedom?"

"What about all those football faces out there?"

"I would say, they fill your and my face-space as many different disguises that we wear. Each and every one of them is the quantum field, did they but see it – and the private movie every instant getting longer. But you've got to be practical too. The hassle doesn't stop – but when your whole standpoint changes, it's bound to get your life out of the rut, you deal with it better. You know you're the unborn winner behind your mask, and the born loser in front? The unborn behind, never dies. Everything filling up the front, passes through and changes, it's just petrol for the car. You can watch. Life is the movie. Live back to front!

"But that reminds me – you want to see Douglas's *bombe atomique*? Wait, I'll show you." Tom cut the bottom of a big brown paper bag so that both its ends were open, a tube. Then he fitted his face into one end with about half an inch around it, for air, and invited Fred to fit his face into the other end.

"Hey, this is going too bloody far!" protested Fred "What're we playing now – Franciscan monks? I might catch something, darling!"

"Wait," said his friend, regardless, "How many faces in this bag? Scientifically – how many faces do you see?"

Fred looked for some time silently. The sides of the paper bag removed his friend's face from the context of everyday things and snide resistances. Bit by bit, he freed himself to gaze and to receive the information as if he had never seen such a thing before. It was rather warm in the paper bag, and from time to time they had to come out, like divers, for air. At first the intimacy embarrassed him. Presently, as Fred agreed in himself to override his frettings, he found himself contemplating with compassion, a living landscape. He received the searchlight of that sensitive terrain into his own. He saw how the pupils and lids of the eyes narrowed or dilated, as they roved and scanned mountains and valleys. They examined features in detail – eyes, nose, the lines in a forehead, the contour of the cheek, the growth of hair or beard, the twitch and lilt of expression. They saw the baby unborn and everlasting, the bed of the river, the vulnerable soul in those dark eyes which, like wells, never age or end: the youthful profundity of that searching glance.

With his own depth, Fred received and beheld an inescapable *mysterium*, a humanity.

"Just the one face," he replied, after about fifteen minutes, removing his from the bag.

"Yes," said Tom. "You're starting to see the point. The YOUNI-VERSE. You can do it with the mirror too."

Origin and Result (Alpha and Omega) of the Stone
From Bas-Relief, Central Porch, Notre Dame, Paris.

(FULCANELLI)

Santa Claus Economy

Once again, Budget time rolled inexorably round to *denouement.* Members of parliament flooded the chamber and the galleries were filled. Every sleepy seat from the country woke up. Rumour was already rife, due to leaks from the rubbish bin of No 11. Some crumpled shreds bearing the legend – "must do something special" and "give a lot" were scavenged from the Chancellor's trash by the hungry press, sellotaped and interpreted. They fuelled the country to expect something outside precedent.

The Chancellor rose cumbersomely to his feet. Many keen eyes suspected that the tumbler to his right hand contained a generous dose of scotch. "Well," he said, lifting his glasses carefully onto his nose and putting them down again, "I am going to inform the House of just the bare bones of my Budget, before we, ahhh, dress the lady."

A wearied titter and some scuffing shoes greeted his sally. Everyone seemed to have heard him, for there was no baa-ing of sheep. The Chancellor peered, and pounced: "Now, ahhh – we have obtained software designed to manage the Economy perfectly without human intervention. Ladies, gentlemen, honourable members, I repeat: *without human intervention.* The brand name is Santa Claus."

If the Chancellor had hoped to create a stir, he got it. It took several minutes for the House to subside.

Quelling some indignant backbenchers with an icy eye, the Chancellor replaced his glasses and made a show of consulting the papers artfully scattered on his desk. He stood up: "Santa Claus has decided to give every citizen over the age of eighteen a capital grant of three hundred thousand pounds. I repeat, three h ..."

"The people," he continued, when the House was relatively subdued again "have been patient through a most difficult time and worked hard. Worked hard. Therefore, Santa Claus has *accurately* concluded that this amount is available per capita, on the basis of the present huge surplus of Civil-service personnel which can therefore be *economized*."

"ORDER! ORDER!" and much banging ensued. If parliament is a mental organ, the parliamentary mind doesn't like to be told it is not entirely indispensable.

"...cut the Gordian knot," the Chancellor was saying, wiping his brow. He raised his voice and his tumbler: "I can also inform you, honourable members and Mr Speaker, that already we have made, er, *arrangements* with most of the EU governments, and with some of the more ahh, *progressive* administrations in the third world, to run their economies also, on Santa Claus. On terms, as will shortly be laid before you which are, ahh, may I say, *highly* advantageous not only to this government but to the tax payer."

Some of the members began to look a little more thoughtful. The hard times were endemic, the recession still in backlash. "The details," said the Chancellor, emptying his tumbler and putting it down before him with a flourish "will be in my green paper to be published, er, shortly. I can tell you in brief: a questionnaire will be sent out to each and every registered voter in the land, requesting him or her to complete as indicated, and to state how he or she wishes to use the grant. And by the way, this initial paperwork will virtually eliminate the need for any more of it, which so encumbers the present system, and will save on all our resources. Some of our er, *greener* members, please take note.

"Each voting citizen will state how they will use the grant. Santa Claus can calculate whether it is possible and will accept, reject, amend, or suggest an alternative. Now," he ploughed on enthusiastically "Suppose, just let us *suppose* a gentleman has stated he requires a new Porsche, an updated virtual-reality package, a villa in the Seychelles, a body make-over and a permanent seat at Wembley, and for the rest of his grant to be put into shares in a privatized national industry, such as inner city transport or egg marketing. Santa Claus will predicate the balance of material consumption, employment and financing in the transaction, and its effects in the networking of all these concerns locally, as on the economy as a whole and er, make the necessary adjustments. Santa Claus will handle the inter-connective web. Mr Speaker, I am sure you would agree on the efficiency of such a Budget."

The House as a whole was rather stunned. The message was revolutionary. From the gallery, a wag called down, "Does Santa Claus play dice?"

"It has already been estimated," said the Chancellor portentously "that due to the disappearance of economic stress, there will be huge savings in the National Health Service. Many illnesses are, ahh, psychosomatic, so the benefit to industry goes without saying. Santa Claus also predicts a dramatic reduction of Home Office spending due to less ahhh, *crime*. Honourable members, ladies and gentlemen, the resources at present locked up in social benefits, will be released!"

The Chancellor paused. The House, not having collected itself, was for the moment as tame as a lamb. He fiddled with his glasses, then put them on again to press his advantage, and took up an oratorical stance: "Who would have believed, my Lords, ladies and gentlemen of the House *and* our friends in the Press, in a *painless* solution? What ordinary intelligence, other than god-like, could monitor the land's economic health holistically from moment to moment, the local interwoven with the National interest, to perpetually update and upgrade, *and* to make the necessary small adjustments which affect *everyone*, with precision? Only a super-Extra-ordinary intelligence, the Santa Claus faculty, could provide this bold and comprehensive solution to our difficulties."

"Mr Speaker, and honourable members of this House, this is the bare outline of my budget, a 'Lady' whom I can promise you will be svelte, but not *lean*. Before I go into the exciting details, I had better tell you ..."

At that moment a scuffle materialized around his desk. An enigmatic piece of paper was passed around with a murmur. The Chancellor seized it without looking and waved it for the House to see. "Ah yes – just what I was expecting. Santa Claus's first blueprint since his initial forecast has been kindly handed to me by my colleague here. Allow me to share with the House this moment of history! Santa Claus says,

"THIS IS THE FIRST TIME AN ECONOMY HAS BEEN MANAGED BY A SIMULATED ERROR AND I SANTA CLAUS AM ABSOLUTELY INCAPABLE OF ERROR ERROR ERROR ERROR ERROR ERROR ERROR ERRORERRORERRORERROR-ERRORERROR ..."

The Chancellor dropped his glasses.

The Captain's Pupil

TO ADVANCE their own frontier, our braver eggheads propose:

"that all manifestation, from atom to galaxy, is conscious, albeit confined to local capacity and sense data."

A worm of philosophical bent, among stems of grass and grains of soil, may so ascertain itself: likewise the planed and polished surface of the table upon which a philosopher writes his thesis. Have not generations of scribes, with its support, applied their viewpoint to the tree from which it was cut? or the woodworm boring into its leg? Lo, we are not things, the faculty declares: nor confined to particles and sub-particles of fluctuating quanta states, we are worm-holes, *unified strings*. In every hierarchic level, connectivity with the *whole* implicit order is given.

Here comes a personal reflection: the musings of a dab of paint in one of Rembrandt's masterpieces. If you have visited the Rijksmuseum in Amsterdam, you will recall a certain altarpiece - the *Night Watch*. A solemn silence pervades this dark room. The well-lit painting on the wall is protected by a stout barrier and uniformed guards. It portrays the night watch militia, led by Captain Banning-Coqu - who commissioned the painting - guarding the town hall during the thirty years war between Holland and Spain. The painting was not popular at that time. Unlike standard portraits in formal poses, these life size figures are captured in a chiaroscuro of vibrant action. The *Night Watch* became controversial, and it spoiled Rembrandt's later career in this genre of painting. The only sounds now heard in the darkened room are the restless feet of visitors.

My life story invites you to reflect upon one dab of dark blue pigment - the Captain's right eye - like a woodworm's advice to the scribe. Look at me now! I am a drop of soft paint, placed by a brush to harden. My surface is not quite even: one edge slightly raised, forms a ridge, like a crescent of the moon. Through this limited sense I overhear remarks of those who gaze upon this great work, whose pupil point I am, right in the centre...

"Of the principal figures, Captain Frans Banning Cocq wears a deep purple-coloured costume with a red, gold-embroidered sash. On the right, a musketeer in red examines his weapon, and further to the right, a drummer in green. Behind the latter figure, an officer in green points to the left. To the left, a musketeer in red charges his weapon. The standard held by the ensign is striped green and yellow; in front of him are two girls in greenish yellow - one carries a cock. Signed 'Rembrandt f.1642'. The picture is inaccurately described by its traditional name: it represents a company of Amsterdam musketeers marching out by daylight - indeed, by sunlight. Of the twenty nine figures, seventeen are musketeers of the second ward of Amsterdam; their names are written on the Baroque shield hung in the background, the Captain being Frans Banning Cocq, and the lieutenant Willem van Ruytenburch. The picture was painted for the Great Hall of the Musketeers' Guild at Amsterdam, and Rembrandt received 1600 florins for it. Various removals of the picture followed in the 18th and 19th centuries, until in 1885 it was hung in the Rijksmuseum. A copy by Gerard Lundens in the National Gallery and a sketch from the picture in a family album of Frans Banning Cocq's (now belonging to a M.de Graeff, The Hague) proves that the picture has been cut down all round (notably on the left to a width of about 20 inches) - no doubt in the 18th century, when it was moved and fitted between two doors."

Ah, my learned and ignorant friends! Lighten up the double Dutch! For a start, your right and left are opposed to my own. So what are "musketeers"? What is a "florin"?

Come close, and see. A black hole receives you openly; where else could I be? I am your eye, while yet apart. I have not seen, nor am likely to see, the Whole, yet this whereof I speak is mine as much as yours. Around and about me, dabs and whorls of paint are placed, all roughly the same texture and thickness. Many overlay others, some are small, some large, some juxtapose, some flow together like a wave; all adhere to the same strings as myself, and each is interwoven with the thread, the ground, the pigment grinder, the play of the brush, the odour of paint left to dry.

I have, along with all my companions, suffered. I have been cleaned with strange chemicals and retouched with prurient hands and varnished with shades of amber obscurity. I know I am essential. Were I not here, the canvas would be unconscious. See, I hand to you my Master's eye, created from His original hand! This inescapable gesture over three centuries, I patented and realised: I am the *Great Work*. Why else would so many people pay good guilders to gaze at me?

But I want to see myself! Am I looking the wrong way? for it is you I see, not my companions to each side - you who present to me my countenance, my consciousness, you who come to life in this room, pass me by, and die. Are you a Captain of this same vast ignorance?

I asked and got your depth description of myself; but your talk of bearded names, sashes, dates and musketry are alien to the passion of my Master within us - his breath:

"I love unconditionally, humanity," he said. *" I work with young and old. There is no escape; I suffer each pupil to come to me as the potter works his clay. I am never unsurprised, nor unrefreshed. These are my life to love, to rediscover, and shape. Every time, my heart breaks and heals. Every time I enter the*

deep, I forget the things people say about each other. I enter your soul, I open your wings and fly. Creation surpasses me; for I am poised on the brush of an Artist beyond my sight."

Through massings of mixed pigment, we suffer ourselves to be discovered in *The Canvas*, by you who call yourselves *historians*! Our Master's brush adheres to strings, warp and weft; and I as he, now gaze upon your brief facial forms that gaze upon me and fade - the lifetimes of my soul. Some of my companions were born with impetuous brush movements, and some had to bear an almost unbearable scrutiny and re-trial. I was one of the latter. Our Master made many attempts to realise me, and I was a fog of dirty rags. One day He stopped, and allowed His brush to discover the point. Here, I ask: *"why do I see – why am I here at all? - not over there?"*; the question, like a child, again is born. For from every place unknown, I surely see.

Transcending the dark circle of my understanding, is my Master's regard, strangely intense, into One he loves. My life is a mutual love offering. How can I move from where I am? How can I not receive you, who pay guilders to stare at me and state your opinion? Nature's precious stones, ground and blent together with a bonding agent and an oil to flow, released the miracle of my chemical composition and molecular structure, deep blue like the sea. May He from whose hand I flowed with difficulty, give me night vision! May the pupil see itself! as He.

My task undying for you all - brushstrokes dark and light from my Master's hand - is the One becoming the many: the many as the One.

the painter's point
strings the play of higher art
upon the Whole.

Perceval Marlowe Goes to a Poetry Class

"POETRY," HE said, regarding his audience with defiance "turns all things to loveliness. It strips the veil of familiarity from the word, and lays bare the naked and sleeping beauty which is the spirit of its forms."

This young man was rather a lark. A heterogeneous cluster of persons had assembled at Cook's Hotel in Albermarle Street, in response to a flier inviting them to hear a case *'In Defense of Poetry'*. This flier was posted in a number of foyers to catch the eye, some weeks ago. Who says poetry needs defending? They came for curiosity. A few were young at heart. Some wore long hair, others the razor. Some were students of political awareness, and others were members of Andrew Liversidge's poetry workshop at the Metropolitan Institute - an annexe of the City Lit – they came for a chortle because the young man, their class-mate, was a reactionary, a black sheep.

No one else knew him. Perceval Marlowe? The name has a ring to it which cannot quite be placed. It crosses an enigmatic Elizabethan dramatist with the tender and secretive country, which undulates through Henley and Wycombe. Grace afflicts and caresses that contour, the stands of tall beeches breathing the west wind's song, the wooded valleys full of tall flowers, the villages, the watering-holes and hidden farms, the naked curve of fields, footpaths and the sky. *England, where is England*? Perceval Marlowe is an old English name; a *parsifal* we lost. But the cow-parsley sour and wild, is growing here, right under your nose! Who needs to travel overseas? But who can see until he hears?

The young man fidgeting paper in a sitting-room of Cook's Hotel is too tall and too uncoordinated in his nervous movements to inspire confidence. His thick red hair grown rather long, betrays an epidermal sensibility to climate. His hands, nail-bitten, become easily angry. His dark eyes dart swift, like a wild creature disturbed. His gestures are petulant, childish. He wears a white collarless shirt, a black donkey jacket and narrow black jeans. This costume alone distinguishes him. But when he began to speak, it changed. His heart exposed, turned golden, poured fire. It quivered like a feathered arrow.

At Andrew Liversidge's poetry workshop in the MI, Percy is considered rather *old-fashioned*. He grubs up archaic words such as "virtue" - give it a rest for chrissakes! Let real poets progress, and leave Perce to his dustbin treasury - he's daft but harmless. Sometimes he stutters. He's a fish out of water - why does he come each week? Sometimes he reads, which is good for a laugh, for his meek and sheepish *prosody*, whatever that means, gets dipped in ink-black fleece – we're the cutting edge! He is live bait for our bright barbs, we tell him how it is *today*.

Andrew Liversidge the tutor has a razor intellect and his finger on the pulse. He edits the with-it quarterly *'Tell Us'*, and handles Perceval Marlowe with some care; he regards him as talented but eccentric. He needs to be fostered. Percy has a long way to go, to get into the postmodernist main-stream which tells it the way it is, and Andrew knows from experience he won't be hurried. Recently, this young maverick showed some signs of promise, of breakthrough into the contemporary idiom, and Andrew's fatherly interest is whetted. Is Perce letting go of his metric nanny's apron strings? His verse has a strange innate liberty, if erratic; a life-blood for *Tell Us* to promote. But it must be garnished, trained, developed!

So "Percy," said Andrew, on a Thursday morning before the meeting at Albemarle Street "have you brought a poem for us today? It's some time since you read."

The classroom for emergent poets was a room without distinction, suited, with its stackable chairs, empty desks and wide window onto the back of Waterloo East station, to the peripatetic educational requirement. Its warm, bland informality was scraped by many feet. Poets of aspiration and arrival pulled out chairs into a rough circle and retrieved xeroxed sheets from plastic bags and holdalls. Some even possessed brief-cases. Percy possessed a rather grubby pocket. "Yes," he said, putting his hand in it, "I've been writing a poem about Liberation." Ah, thought Andrew. The paper was heavily scored and over-written like those of the other students: Andrew believed that "work in progress" should show the scars. "I've been writing," Percy continued jerkily "this verse over the last day or two and am not, well, very sure about it, I would like some feedback." He detached at last a bundle of creased photocopies from an assortment of keys, knotted handkerchiefs and old Underground tickets, and passed some of them round. Then he sat back, dusted some crumbs from his copy, withdrew into himself and read in a voice now focused - a strange voice it was, unexpectedly deep with a rough edged resonance and the hint of a west-country accent:

"Within a cavern of man's trackless spirit
is throned an image so intensely fair
that the adventurous thoughts that wander near it
worship, and as they kneel, tremble and wear
the splendour of its presence, and the light
penetrates their dreamlike frame
'till they become charged with the strength of flame."

There was a long pause.

"Um. I'm appalled, Percy," said his tutor "After all your years in this class, you're still attempting I see, these rather high flown metaphors which I dare say mean something to you. Any comments?"

"Yes," said Nadya, an energetic essayist from Edgware, "what a forced rhyme - *spirit* and *near it*. Wouldn't *of merit* do better?

"The adventurous thoughts that ferret," said Robert Taskmaster from Hampstead, who took notes and got a laugh.

"Seriously," Nadya pressed on "how can 'dreamlike forms' be 'charged with flame'? It would all catch fire! Sorry Percy, I don't catch on, myself - I'm more down to earth. Can you clarify."

"In words of one syllable," said Percy, "no."

He fell silent. "You either see it - are it - or you don't. Hear it, I mean. Hear it. You know ..."

"Perhaps one might do better to Fear It, Percy my love," said Jonathan, a promising and unemployed graduate. "or do I have to grin and Bear It?"

Thomas the retired schoolmaster crossed and recrossed his knobbly shanks and stabbed a forefinger at his copy; his voice was slow and genial "This rhyming scheme doesn't work. It forces the meaning. Why have you abandoned free verse? Besides, you've got no rhyme for 'light', have you."

"He's spared us that," said Mrs Wansy, a vicar's wife.

"Oh no he hasn't. Spirit and It!" There were groans.

"I don't think we need spend more time on this, Percy," remarked

Andrew Liversidge expeditely, for the class was losing aesthetic focus "Is this what you expected? Why not continue with that rather interesting tale of Peter Bell you read us a few weeks ago. Now, Liz, can we have something from you?"

Liz Levy, a well known figure in some low-budget magazines and pub pentameter readings, had two slim volumes to her credit. She was vociferously successful on the cultural fringe, and of good Muswell Hill stock, gone independent. Her stalwart shawled figure was crowned with a mane of dark frizzed hair, heavy eyebrows and specs with steel hexagonal rims. Lightly, she produced from her bag some bright white sheets from her PC, passed them round, playfully put out her tongue and read:

DEMI TASSE

"When i park ass in the Mocha shop
my Him of bliss
is your instant coffee blend
folks, our thirstful granules coagulate,
brewed, roasty and frig frozen
demi-tasse so hot
caffeinate, head strong simulate
jive Java baby, frothy!"

"Just a moment, my dear," said Andrew. "Now Percy, why can't you write like Liz, you have the ability. Look how she uses a metaphor, really rams it home. Go on, Liz."

"Sipping steamy mix
Cappucino! i cried orgasmatically
and then like bean arabesque
grown wild on mountain peak
ground in his grinder to gold dust

filter, rammed in cafetiere dramatically
espresso'd black and dark, pour cream
on me baby, i cried, i cried ecstasis!

"Drink me, java baby,
stir me with your spoon,
pour into me your sugar, you turk
to taste
jive java baby frothing soon!
dont leave me on the mountain top!
gimme java baby jive,
jive java baby O!"

The class smacked its lips. "Now that is *poetry*. Sheer passion. Telling it the way it is."

"I really like Liz's intensity," echoed Gilda, who was married to an Adlerian analyst "It could be sung to rap!"

"Rather an interesting blend of Java and Turkish - I don't think I've tried it, Liz," remarked Thomas "but I'm not sure about that word orgasmatically."

"When it comes to the crotch," said Nadya, "who cares? it hits the fan. It bursts into flavour, Liz. It's good, it shouldn't be grammatical."

"Orgasmatic, automatic. A pun on the advertising. "

"Yeah, great title. Read it again, Liz."

When she had done so, Percy had a question. "Is he real? Great energy, crisp and black, but are you really there?"

"What exactly do you mean?" said Liz

"Like a song before the bird comes, do you wait, do you open your ... you know?"

"Know what? – no I DON'T - it's spontaneous, baby. Don't get heavy. Why?"

"I can't tell you," said Percy, flushing and inarticulate again "you got to wait a bit, not drive it all yourself. It's just ... oh never mind."

Thomas the retired schoolmaster, was invited to read next. "I'm off," said Percy standing up "I'm going to meet - oh, never mind. By the way, I am speaking on Sunday evening, 7.30 at Cook's in Albermarle Street. Any of you want to come?"

As Perceval left the building, to walk the street till he came into focus, he bit his knuckles, his eyes darted a bit wildly from side to side. Couldn't he have expressed that better? Why does the voice of the maid desert him, just as he feeds her to the swine? Oh it's obvious! But *why come* to the tip of his tongue, only to drop, betray and break the holy vessel? *Receive* ... Shouldn't he be thankful she flees the moment his inner ear is poised to *tell her as she is*? Her scent wells up to the hot mix, and the crossfire in the poetry class abandons her.

His very own Emily, his intimate treasure, should be defended and protected. His dragon pride guards her within the deep-briar dingle, his pride smarts, burns, and cannot be trusted not to rust. Follow the red knight - a gleam of ruddy fire in his inner eye just now eluded him! Where is it? The knight shining scarlet galloped away into a veil of white silver-birch stems in the forest, leaving him unhorsed. Every bright sinew, each slender tree is strung on a harp the summer breeze softly soughs. It is August and almost his birthday. The gods gave him, a Leo, a fomidable pair of protagonists to wrestle the royal poets' art. The same lion and serpent in his dreams, appeared to his legendary hero of the Graal, Sir Perceval of Arthurian Wales, who was abandoned on an island of testing solitude. Dreadfully the creatures fought, and stormed the sea.

Through the fellowship of the Table Round, Sir Perceval struggled to perfect himself. Victoriously, he lost everything, and remembered his fiery Cross in the nick of time. The innocent boy, on the verge of erring, remembered the Lord, when all the thickets on the hill burst into red flame. He knew that he, though shamefully unhorsed, would find and follow the trail within him. Not even in his *Defense of Poetry* may this point of fire be revealed. Only with Emily, his girl who, hidden in the dark wood awaits him softly nude, may he share it, for they to each other are the fire. Nobody knows of Emily. Percy's gossip page harbours fictional heroines and liaisons. He wraps a dark mantle of "Mystery Dramas" and political reformation, around the inward pearl he guards, so rapt.

Pacing a greying pavement of parked cars, Percy distils a fresh sentence for his *Defense of Poetry*, toys with, memorises and quickly makes a biro note on the back of the folded copies of *Man's Trackless Spirit* in his pocket: *"It purges from our inward sight the film of familiarity which obscures from us the wonder of our being."* Only poetry can save the world from its appearances. The Underground station arrived with its friendly red and blue circle for a game of snakes and ladders, and he ran downstairs into its dark mouth and was hidden.

"Follow to the deep woods' weeds, the wildbriar dingle ..."

Perceval has a familiar, whose name of course is Marlowe.

Marlowe may be found wherever Nature grows tall, adorned with old mans' beard and wild flowers. The furry ponds of Sussex, the rolling Chiltern contour with beech garlands, the elusive Camelot of mid Wales, are all the same to his all-weather dishevelment; for Marlowe's one duty is to tramp, to keep no roof over his head. In vagabond pastures, Marlowe *watches* the dragon who guards a pearl. He knows yon dragon's times for resting and for fire-breathing, and beckons the children to come and see; shows them also stars of morning dew that cling to the leaves, shows them where the cave is hidden behind the rock. If they can find some fresh dewy grass for thirsty dragon to drink, the children may leave him to his joy and enter the cool cave.

Old Marlowe can do nothing with their secret - he can only show the way. He sleeps out in it, is rained and crept upon, and burnt by sun and frozen by frost; a weather-beaten scarecrow, a little light in the head, gruff in country speech, festooned with clematis tendrils. Suddenly, uncouthly he appears, where cloistered dark oaks meet a bright open field, all wet he is with undergrowth and slugs. He shows the children how to play with fire, stalk ghosts and brew outlandish chemistries in a blackened pot. Merlin himself may have taught him, but Marlowe being rather simple and repeatedly sun-struck, has forgotten all save a very few simple spells. He is the writer of Perceval's "Mystery Play". Once upon a time, he knew what the stars told, but it is all now hearsay.

"Do you hear it?" Perceval Marlowe remembered now, through the sustained hoot of the train in the tunnel, what he was trying to say to Liz. Do you, does your lover when he has you, ever keep still, to hear ... wait, with the silent sea sound, and let the earth-angel speak? or does he, excited egotistical fool, rush the fence? Percy wrestles the angel of his submission with every stanza, rhyme or speech. Do you hear the lark rise when you lie on your back in a field? Who holds the pencil ... ah, he lost it again! still trying to think it through. It ripples, rocks him like a wave, a musical pulse, the wind's song, a metre trips forth, the dance came first and then the words ... but this is no good 'till he gives himself up to be its disciple. Willing to be still, he hears ... the Will. He wept to be done. This sort of thing won't divide up or fit into classes; for his own crusty exterior, he chooses to be a religious iconoclast. In this age he is born, icons are broken, the pebbles in young David's sling are broken, not aimed; it is all well meaning, but to what avail? They all are prisoners breaking rocks, and they think they are letting themselves out of the bag!

He, Perceval, keeps game in the forest, and for a moment he struts about and re-shapes his speech to Liz: "Do you, darling, ever fuck? Really? Have you heard behind your ear, did you tune your fork to your lover, or do you just tell it how *you* think it is...?" - No, no, won't do, can't say or hear it, save with one who is cracked the same way. Blessed are the cracked, for they let in the light ... He fears greatly his own exposure, his being improperly made.

There is one golden rule to write with. Be still and listen; follow the wave, the quaver as it comes, being sensitive to higher association. Let it surprise like dawn before cock crows; and let it perfect itself, be a patient polisher of the pulse, the hidden gleam that rhymes within, 'til the sky within the cavern speaks ... *spirit hear the sun rise, sunrising, hear it say, the river, the stream, stake me, let me pour forth abundantly*. The legs and arms of his lovely Emily are around him laughing on the grassy ground. The train stopped with a jerk at Goodge Street. Perceval Marlowe stepped out onto the bright-lit platform vaguely singing, and disappeared up a channel to the street. Let it well. Say "Well well well ... a well", then stay by the well, say nowt, and see what wells up. Today's class of poets gives them things to do, too soon.

"Liz, he's sensational! he scratches your skin – so tasty! Mine is Love! she undoes me - not hasty!" Towards perfect pitch with the gold-rush instant blend, there are discords. Perceval is a very young man and he finds it very hard to control himself. He has a mad temper on him and is prone to trembling. He loves to eat oysters, sip their juice and throw away their shells. It is lunch time now. Oh Emily, what joy.

In his mind the Rubaiyat chimed:

> *"There was a Door to which I found no Key;*
> *There was a Veil past which I could not see;*
> *Some little Talk awhile of ME and THEE*
> *There seemed - and then no more of Thee and Me ..."*

and his interior voice began also to provide another draft:

> "Did you dare to undress by the well, the offering?
> to lie on the hill at night, and bathe in streams?
> to tumble midst mud and rose, to search and sing? -
> The quaver in a stormy star, the lion redeems!

To he whose soul is born of fire, the poet of a thousand songs, may he go forth!

Sunday evening at Cook's in Albemarle Street found Perceval Marlowe addressing a small gathering of curious spirits in the suite that his income - sources unknown - had mysteriously hired for him. Liversidge, Gilda and a few others from the class went along to amuse themselves. In the name of progress, wheels within wheels are turning. And some of the wheels have wheels of their own.

"In the name of English poetry," said Perceval Marlowe

suddenly and without warning, standing to his full height and throwing back his red hair "I now speak facts."

The tired furniture of the room stood still. Percy's white shirt opened, his tight black trousers quivered, his eyes were pouncing cats, his long straight nose and intensely pale cheeks glowed; like a leopard, he gathered to leap. His presence struck a rustle of fear, a breath of flame, they had to hear.

"Can any of you say," said he in his strange disembodied voice whose quaint country resonance soared like an eagle "what is Imagination?" He looked around. "Here are three definitions of this word. The first from a dictionary in 1799: *'A power or faculty of the Soul to marry or separate impressions the senses receive, in such manner as to form creative compounds.'* The second from today's Shorter Oxford English Dictionary: *'the action of forming a mental concept of what is not actually present to the senses.'* The third, from the ancient world: *'to separate the subtle from the gross, with prudence, humility and good judgement; to ascend in your heart with deep wisdom from Earth to Heaven; then again descend to Earth and unite the powers of Above and Below'.* My friends, which of these definitions has spunk?"

Silence.

"Imagination," he went on " a word containing *image, the magus, magic, power,* is a faculty of the Soul to bind and loose what she receives from the senses, all five of 'em, to create new beings, to let them make love, make children, go forth. I put it to you, that a more common definition for the imagination these days, is "fanciful" – just fancy this and fancy that, but it's all infancy. Who truly imagines? Who creates reality? Call him a magus, a poet. Acting within the hidden cause of his calling, he cherishes the effect that is born. Bright ripple go forth, the musical measure, the master key - bathed in its source, wood, field, mountain, why confine to the towns' flattery? He's a knight of the Grail. She is the soul. True to him, as he to her, is the art of love, of chivalry unrivalled.

"In their defense, I will share with you now some extracts from my Essay *'In Defense of Poetry'*. "

He picked up some sheets, but exultantly knew most of it by heart, and all but extempore, addressed the room:

"If our age of Reason, my friends, is the faculty of the mind to distinguish its own parts, the fact of Imagination is mind's volition itself, to act upon as within those parts, and colour them with its light.

Reason enumerates all the differences.
Imagination weds and beds the similitudes.
The inert body of Reason to the flambant spirit of Imagination is as shadow to the substance.
So what is poetry?
My friends, poetry is the expression of Imaginative power!

"Man is an Aeolian lyre or field of long summer grass.
He is driven to ripple, to sway, to resonate melody.
What is that innate conscious principle? –
it acts upon these strings of his heart, his life, his joy, his grief and fears.
It seeks to adjust sound or motion thus excited,
it seeks to derive from them not melody alone, but harmony...."

***

"... It must turn all things to loveliness.
It exalts the beauty of that which is most beautiful.

It adds beauty to that which is most deformed.
It marries exultation to horror, grief and pleasure, to eternity and change.
It subdues to unity under its light yoke, all irreconcilable things.
It transmutes all that it touches.
Every form moving within its radiance is changed by sympathy to an incarnation of the spirit,
the presence which it breathes.
Its secret alchemy turns to potable gold the poisonous waters, which flow from earth through life.
It is stripping the veil of familiarity from the world.
It is laying bare the naked and sleeping beauty which is the spirit of its forms."

The young man paused, stood quite still for a moment, his eyes saw not any one person, but something shone from them. The golden bird was trembling. You could hear a pin drop. He went on:

"As Milton wrote: 'The mind is its own place, and of itself can make a heaven of hell, a hell of heaven.' But pure poetry defeats the curse which binds us to be subjected to the accident of surrounding impressions. Whether it spreads its own figured curtain or withdraws life's dark veil from before the scene of things, it equally creates for us a being within our being. It reproduces and irradiates the common universe of which we are portions and percipients.

"My friends! Poetry purges from our inward sight that film of familiarity which obscured from us the wonder of our being!

"Of what kind are the greatest poets?
Surely, men of virtue, a consummate prudence.
"If we could but look into the interior of their lives, we might find they were the most fortunate of men.

"Why? For they are compelled only to serve the Power
which is seated upon the throne of their own Soul.

"Such true poets measure the circumference and sound the depth of
human nature.
The spirit of their quest is comprehensive and all-penetrating.
They are the most sincerely astonished; for it is less their spirit than
the spirit of the age.
They are hierophants of an unapprehended inspiration.
They are the mirrors of gigantic shadows which futurity casts upon
the present.
They are the words which express what they understand not yet.
They are the trumpets which sing to battle, knowing not what they
inspire.
They are the subtle influence which, moving not, moves all things.
They are unacknowledged legislators of the World.
They illumine then, our times.
Facing the responsibility, deeming themselves unworthy, they
redeem."

"The poet" he said, with some defiance, looking at them with his
hands on hips, "turns all things to loveliness. Let me now leave
you with my Aeolian:

**FROM ODE TO THE WEST WIND, CIRCA 1819 BY PERCY BYSSHE
SHELLEY**

Make me thy lyre, even as the forest is:
what if my leaves are falling like its own!
The tumult of thy mighty harmonies

will take from both a deep autumnal tone
sweet, though in sadness. Be thou, Spirit fierce
my spirit! Be thou me, impetuous one!

Scatter as from an unextinguished hearth
ashes and sparks, my words among mankind!
Be through my lips to unawakened Earth

the trumpet of a prophecy! O Wind
if Winter comes, can Spring be far behind?

Sir Perceval stepped down, sheathed his sword and quaffed his fire in a large glass of water. He was a gangling and shaken young man again. The members of Liversidge's poetry workshop rose and in solidarity left the room in Cook's Hotel without waiting for the cheers that broke out from Percy's young and motley audience.

***

The following Thursday, Perceval Marlowe arrived as usual at class.

"Well," said his tutor "that was quite a tirade you gave us, Percy. Quite the young firebrand, eh? Some of us might question the relevance of such romantic sentiments to contemporary cultural facts. I wonder about your political maturity. So what have you brought today?"

"I didn't think you would get the point," said his student "so I have abandoned that stanza in my poem on Liberation I read last week, but have substituted these." Another pile of typescript emerged from his capacious black pocket and was distributed. With a distant air, Percy read out loud:

Come Thou, but lead out of the inmost cave
of man's deep spirit, as the morning-star
beckons the Sun from the Eoan wave
wisdom. I hear the pennons of her car
selfmoving, like cloud charioted by flame;

comes she not, and come ye not,
rulers of eternal thought ...

***

"... as a wild swan, when sublimely winging
its path athwart the thunder smoke of dawn,
sinks headlong through the aerial golden light
on the heavy sounding plain
when the bolt has pierced its brain;
As summer clouds dissolve, unburthened of their rain;
as a far taper fades with fading night,
as a brief insect dies with dying day,
my song, its pinions disarrayed of might
drooped; o'er it closed the echoes far away
of the great voice which did its flight sustain,
as waves which lately paved his watery way
hiss round a drowner's head in their tempestuous play."

"Sorry," he said abruptly "I can't wait for your comments. I have to meet my publishers."

Joyously he sketched a farewell salute and ran lightly from the building to enter his wood. He tuned his thought to the IAMbic strings. Like a quiver of deep ocean it flowed. He found Emily. Her indigo shell to him opened. Her pearl was a rainbow shimmering in high summer around him as his arrow flamed.

"Follow to the deep wood's weeds,
follow to the wild-briar dingle
where we seek to intermingle
and the violet tells her tale
for they two have enough to do
of such work as I and you."

The Sphinx

Herr Doktor David Wiseacre adjusted his pince-nez. Carefully, he set his right palm under his bearded chin, and placed his elbow firmly on his oak desk, forming a pedestal like Rodin's *Le Penseur*.

One can almost hear the mental machinery grinding. Finely tuned electronics whirr in his furrowed brow. A trapped fly buzzes up and down the window pane; he is oblivious – the professor ponders the pendulum between points of view.

Dr.Wiseacre is the highly respected Professor Emeritus of advanced Metaphysics at the ancient University of Tubingen. He is the pride of the German academic establishment. They regard him as a genius, arguably the most outstanding since Albert Einstein, whom by comparison, many have considered a bit of a dolt. Some even believe he's a reincarnation of the great Immanuel Kant, the Sage of Magdeburg. World opinion has held that he outshone all his predecessors in the noble tradition of Western hyper-idealism. His book *The Core Questions Beyond Paranormal Metaphysics* was hailed as a universal masterpiece, a superb 'a priori intellectualisation' of the highest order. There had been nothing like it since the 'Critique of Pure Reason'.

For certain reasons best known to him, three years ago Dr Wiseacre chose to abandon all this excitement, and to make his home in London. Perhaps the celebrity has palled. A study of the Stoics directed him to a more austere environment, where he could enjoy the Recession. He was recommended to a villa overlooking Holders Hill Park; she keeps a kosher house. The rent was rather high, and the room needs decorating, but his bursary is generous; he settled immediately, and enriched his reflections on the home ground of Bacon's English School, whose distinguished heirs – Locke, Berkeley, Hume and Russell – have further teased western thought along those diligent generations. Indeed, he occasionally leaves his desk to stroll into the park and enjoy the air. For from the window of his back bedsitter, a prospect of green meadows, a rolling golf course and seminars of graceful, feathered trees, extending to a good-natured horizon, invites him.

But to-day the Professor is glum and down cast, behind the glass. His native Teutonic abstractions have the upper hand, and his head aches. He has collided with a great problem which threatens to undermine the magnificent cast iron structure of his conceptual linguistic analysis – his lifetime's work. A worm is eating him! Recently, he began to suspect that this world in which he lives, has no substantial or material reality whatsoever. What is more, he is the only so called 'mind', and he exists in some kind of weird phantasmagorical dream! This notion won't go away, and it is upsetting him. The fine view from the window is all in the mind. A fly is buzzing – *ach!*

He pondered some more, and then suddenly moved over to his Toshiba and began to briskly bang the keys. These will be his preparatory notes for the address he will deliver to the conference on the "Ultimate State of Consciousness Studies". It is being held in honour of the great Arthur Schopenhauer, no less, this coming summer in Geneva.

He wrote:

"AM I THE SOLE DREAMER?

SOME FOOD FOR COLLEAGUE DREAM FIGURES IN MY DREAM TO PONDER

"I believe that I am pure infinite absolute consciousness-awareness-bliss. That is my true nature, or the Self."

Nah! Nein! he thought, pushing back his chair. *Das ist not gutt. Whoever told you that? Locke has held that the ...* At that moment, something soft brushed his calf; he started, looked down and saw his landlady's cat Sabina, tail in the air. *She gets in through the bathroom window.* "Go, go away, pussy!" He read the sentence again, without comprehension, tried to concentrate, but found his mind wandering; his hands tapped out:

"... Unfortunately this primordial truth has been obscured by my many latent egotistic tendencies accumulated in this and possibly previous lives.

"However, I know that I exist. This causes the light of my pure Consciousness to arise and to mirror these latent tendencies and egotism. Therefore, the world, body, and mind that appear to me are actually unreal, like some dream projected on my screen of pure Consciousness. Am I therefore the sole dreamer of that dream? Are the so called 'others' merely dream figures in my preordained dream of life?"

The professor struck the "Save" key, and leaned back in his creaky chair. *This is arguably an accurate proposition. The cat Sabina is pulling his trouser leg; she is about to leap up into his lap.* When he first moved in to Mrs Felsenberg's, Sabina was still a kitten, and absently he allowed her to sit on his knee while he was working; the tapping keys became her lullaby; absently also, he would stroke her while wrestling a difficult point. *Now he can't get rid of her!* Grudgingly, he gave in, for it is too much trouble to break his thread, and put her out. *She leaps, scrabbles, lands, and kneads his thin thighs with her claws while she rotates, to settle her bed.* Ach! Ow! Stoically, he endures.

Systematically she subsides, and purrs. The professor's mind races on:

"This is not exactly a philosophic solipsism, such as the famed Bishop George Berkeley and others propounded 'de novo'. It is much more sophisticated.

"2. A WARNING
While still holding onto the 'I am the sole Dreamer' notion, keeping it in mind, I must always live and behave as if the apparent dream and the dream figures I seem to perceive are other than myself, and therefore real. The dream figures are conditioned in my predetermined dream world to react aggressively, if my behaviour does not conform with what is regarded as 'normality' by them; i.e. if I do not act as if their dream world was Real.

The dream world imposes consequences on the 'sole dreamer' who does not conform to its predetermined character, or behave as if it was real. Such is the nature of this mental delusion."

He paused again. Now he is far away among the distant trees. He is stroking Sabina's soft fur, again and again, rhythmically. Her pleasure warms his fingertips and palm. The sensation barely registers cognitively; yet sensuously it prevails. Abstract cognition is his freedom. She quietens and prepares his mind. A range of snowy mountains excitingly beckons him; like a chamois he leaps from crag to crag. The cat stretches, yawns sharp teeth, flexes claws again. From the accomplices in pleasure, the web spins on and on ...

"3. SOLIPSISTIC DELUSION
"Solipsistic delusion is one of the powers inherent in the organ of cognition - to delude the human being, that the so called world appears as a dream or hallucination – a mountain, a cloud or a lump

in the ground. This is because, built into the organ of my cognition, brain and senses, are a priori conditioned reflexes of Time, Space and Causality. Every sentient being creates his or her own universe, from the mosquito to the chimpanzee, according to the structure of its organ of cognition ..."

What? A childhood memory is knocking at the door. His mother told him that a stoat and a weasel are - *ach*, then what was it?

"In the human being, the inbuilt mechanism of space creates the three dimensional theatre or screen of consciousness on which the pre-programmed dream unfolds. This unfolding of 32 frames a second in perception, gives an impression of events happening in a temporal sequence like a cinema film. It is compounded by the observation of changes apparently taking place, in the so called natural forces, as seen in this life dream. The causal faculty deduces a reason for these so called 'happenings', which may be accurate or inaccurate. The 'me' acts accordingly in response."

He is still searching – that enticing little valley – yes! That visit to the fortifications at the end of Brean Down. He was a child, on holiday with his parents in the English west country. The wartime fort is rusted by the sea; in spring the returning swallows swoop down Brean and skim the Bristol Channel waves, as they skid home like arrows, to Wales. He and his brother Benjamin played the siege of Sebastopol through concrete bunkers cracked by dandelions; and at the iron door of one of these, he stood looking out cautiously to each side; for his brother hunted him. In the fall of sour grass, broken bricks and rubbish across the path, he detected a tiny movement – a small head by a hole – two bright eyes; it quivered and vanished.

"Mother! Mother! I saw a stoat!"

"What's the difference," asked Benjamin, coming up and grabbing him, "between a stoat and a weasel? How do you tell them apart? Bang, you're dead!"

Their mother was English, so she replied, "You can *weaselly* tell them apart, *liebchen*, because a stoat *is-totally* different."

Upon this premise stands the Professor's life work. The unanswerable conundrum pops out from his hole. The emotional sterility of his limited cogitation disintegrates, and he is a child again.

At the end of Brean Down, a sleeping serpent sinks into the sea. Among the stones, a little stoat is seen. He sees us with his eyes, and disappears into a hidey hole. But what really does he see? And what is concealed behind the forms of nature that we see?

Delighted with this pictorial potential – how it will flummox his students! - the Professor smoothes his forefinger along the cat's whiskers. Perhaps there's a drop of milk in the fridge – perhaps it hasn't gone sour?

The human visual spectrum is one slice off the pie of reality, one sliver cut across the apple, the total universe called Adam. But what of the total universe called Stoat? The Professor is on the horns of a dilemma – to disturb the cat and fetch a sardine for her from the cupboard, or to pursue the pleasure of his thoughts, and her bliss. How can I know, he wonders, in a rare mood of softness, what she sees in me. Am I a biped? Or a heavy yet benevolent pair of paws through the feline filter? How can I know what the small russet stoat sees and reacts to? Or whether he knows the difference between seeing and being in his hole? Or what his own point, in the relative world which I think of as Brean Down, can possibly feel like? I KNOW NOTHING!

NOTHING! And yet I contemplate myself. All appearance, all matter, all that matters and all that does not, floats like clouds or water-lily leaves in front of the tremendous space of manifestation.

This paragraph floats through the Professor's busy mind and leaves not a trace; for he is on his feet, and fussing around the fridge; the cat Sabina, after a brief lick to save her face, now preens against her expected treat. She is a handsome animal, with a pure white face, black ears and black saddles along her back. Her tail, thick and shiny like a wet otter, is erect with joy. "There you are!" exclaims the Professor, stroking her – he found an old bit of cheese also, which she seeks to like. And now, to return to the problem ...

"4. NOTES ON THE DREAM OF SUFFERING IN AN UNREAL WORD
All the dream figures complain endlessly and bitterly about the immense amount of suffering which appears to happen in their individual dream of the world. But the world cannot be judged horizontally, just as it seems to appear on their screen of consciousness. It is better perceived vertically, as a densely populated field of Fate, where the hand of preordained destiny is constantly directing these dream figures to actions, which are designed ultimately for them to pursue their selfish egotistic pleasures."

Sabina has finished her snack, and is doing her toilette.

"These dream figures interact all the time unknowingly. A world of suffering appears as a consequence; but internally they are being taught a severe lesson which forces them to turn within introspectively, and end their dreadful repetitive cycle of dream births. Then aid arrives, and relief descends in the form of an enlightened

Philosopher like me, who reveals certain teachings, or ways to escape from the prison house of their dreams."

The Professor pauses. The cat eyes him speculatively. Then he continues:

"But they must work persistently on themselves. Self-investigation and Self-interrogation help to remove all their old latent habits and conditioned tendencies, which create their dreams. Then the Real Self shines through. The suffering soul wakes up to Reality, and the dream ends."

The Professor is now boiling himself a cup of tea in a saucepan on the Baby Belling; he ransacks the drawer for biscuits. Sabina has gone off in a dignified huff. He feels sleepy, abandons the Toshiba and lies down on the bed for a nap.

"5. MORE ON THE DREAM FIGURES
To imagine that there are ' some others who are real' in the dream of life, is like imagining that all the dream figures in one's private night dream are dreaming the same dream as you are, at exactly the same time.

"6. FIRST PERSON EVENTS
Only one's own first person events have any validity. We have no experience whatsoever of another's first person events. We only interpret them by inference, which is widely open to misinterpretation by us, and cannot be relied upon with any exactitude. The 'other' can only be interpreted as a 'dream figure' because we have no reliable experiential evidence of his or her actual existence or consciousness, except as dreamed by us, which is then superimposed by us upon him or her.

"We are left with being the Sole Dreamer until realisation of the real

Self unveils the illuminated substrate of the world. This may be perceived as Real and is no longer a subjective dream."

The Professor lay dreaming about The Indifferent One. The Indifferent One, he was told, is I and Thou. The Indifferent One looks out of each and all of our eye sockets, uniquely. The bone is its container, and the Indifferent One wanders in and out of the orbital cavities at will ... through a fluid co-incidence of Will, within as without, to be done. On the fourth day of the vision of Christian Rosenkreutz, a white serpent wound herself about through the eye-holes of a skull ... An old book on anatomy for artists was in his hand. Why! Here's a drawing of the skull – and each gaping socket for the eye is a base of a pyramid with four faces – and the apex of two pyramids points inward to cranial centre! The apex is Quintessence – the point of "5" within the four elements. No need to cross your eyes! The 5 is an Egyptian priest. He co-ordinates the quickening mystery of earth and heaven. It comes to focus through the apex. It receives also rain, and lightning.

"And look, my own orbital pyramids point inward. My brain streams visual stimuli along the optic nerve into each apex, to perceive - outward through the widening bony base - the earthly world. The further in I look, the wider appears the world outside. And I begin to ask Who is looking in? – through the vault to heaven? And so the mystery of Five in the magic square of Three is plain to me as the breath of life moves in and out of my solar plexus. The mystery of Five in the magic Square of Three, with equal intervals to each side, is my instrument of vision. It enters and then seems to emanate from somewhere within the depth of my noddle. God be in my head, and in my ... nein, nein! wrong religion, dumkopf ... "

He further reflects,

"Who am I? The Sphinx asks that question. The Sphinx's gaze is the mill or wheel on which the grain is pounded and the loaf is kneaded. The great Eliphas Levi has said, 'Angels not wholly freed, fall again into the abyss.'

"From the Sphinx's gaze within, my mask of life begins to slip and crumble away from bedrock, like peeling paint. It leaves a cave or cavity – like water or air. The Sphinx appears pitiless, but only relatively so, from the lower levels. Through the Sphinx, I actually am the pounding of the provincial grain upon the wheel. At certain shy moments, the intense calm of the Sphinx's smile ... I look out through these caves, in the mountain of sandstone that this great cat is.

Her smile is a deep, central peace – my dreamless sleep – the gentle airs. There is no movement at the hub of the wheel. Those who are subjected to Her gaze, live and die upon Her anvil. But those who are equal to Her gaze begin to learn to love their enemies. In the Bull and the Lion of Ezekiel's vision, dwell in unity the Eagle and the Angel – the serpent Redeemer. 'Whenever you meet someone, think deeply: 'G-d - The HOLY ONE - dwells in this body. Then comes initiation for ever.'" Initiation through so "Indifferent" a "One", wakes from the dream, always.

The Professor started from his slumber, hurried to his disheveled desk, woke up the Toshiba, and wrote firmly:

"7. OBJECTION
Most important Philosophers state that the case for Solipsism is formidable. The chief objection however, comes from Arthur Schopenhauer, whom we honour to-day. He says that 'the object necessarily implies a subject'. But as the subject supplies the object, as has already been stated by me, this fails.

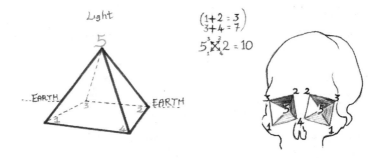

THE MAGIC SQUARE OF THREE

4	9	2
3	5	7
8	1	6

Three-squared (3X3) is 9. The digits of each row, across, vertical or diagonal, add up to 15 (3X5). Of further interest, are the intervals radiating from 5, to the pairs of numbers to each side. And so on …

"8. GENERAL OBSERVATIONS

Ludwig Wittgenstein believed that Solipsism is at the core of the Metaphysical. Even the Subject's relationship to Philosophy and other Philosophers is a solipsistic experience. It is impossible to get beyond the boundaries of the egotistic self, until one realises pure Consciousness. What evidence is there of a World beyond our mental states, other than the deceptive senses, which are all highly untrustworthy? To infer there is a world from other dream figures' statements is nonsensical, as it begs the question of 'who makes the inference?' The subject, and the reply from the object, the dream figure, is supplied by me, the sole dreamer, myself."

"But I," he ruminated, "am not a stoat. The stoat is not a David Wiseacre. Both of us are potentially weasels, and neither of us is the cat. *Nein, Nein!*" For congestion threatened to overwhelm him in its dry harbours. He grabbed his cap and coat and hurried downstairs out of doors. From his landlady's sombre back garden, a little latch-gate gave access to the Park. Next door, in Hendon Cemetery, hosts of rank anxieties lay at last in stony peace; on such occasions, that regimented garden, battered and be-mossed by the four seasons, soothed him.

But the sun was beginning to set, tinting the whole western sky orange beyond the sparse and disciplined woodlands. And the first thing the Professor saw, as he stepped past the oak tree and out onto the cut grass, was the cat. Sabina sat in the long grass at the foot of the tree, quite, quite still, with the setting sun in her face, and ignored him; she sat like a Queen. So he stopped, for his flight from philosophy had made him breathless. He stopped, and watched. He had noticed a certain tension.

Presently the cause of this came into view. *Liebe Gott!* A most remarkable animal. It came over the links, creeping nearer and nearer to Sabina's wide ring-pass-not, as if bewitched. It was tall, it had a cat-like grace, it stalked, it glided on slender, sinewy silver legs, feathered a little with long white hairs; it had a long, slender muzzle, soft dark eyes like a seal in a fairy tale, and an improbable tail held high, bushy and silky soft like a squirrel – this animal was pure white all over, and shone in the slanting light; this animal was A DOG. The Professor trembled, and stood rooted to the spot. Along the animal's curving spine, all the short hairs stood up in tufts, even as far as the splendid tail. And it prowled, from side to side, like a serpent or metaphysical break-through ; for Sabina held her field. Like an Egyptian priestess, her spell enshielded her to a distance of at least ten metres; silently she hissed; the invader as silently opened his jaws to snarl, but couldn't bark. No mythological creature such as this, can merely bark. The space was electrically charged. Were they at play, or were they predators? Suddenly it exploded. The dog broached an invisible wire; Sabina turned and shot up the tree, like lightning in reverse, and sat in the first high fork, as wise, as feathered and unblinking as AN OWL – the brilliance of the sunset in her face.

And the Professor could do nothing. "*Dubi!*" A human biped from beyond his line of sight, called to the animal, who pranced a little, obeyed the distraction, and reluctantly loped away. The Professor stood in the grass, unable even to think of fetching a ladder; because Nature knows how Cheshire cats get there, and Nature knows how to get down again, and his dream is not permitted to interfere. He walked a little away, and in the oak tree still shone that white brilliant star, defiantly aloft. It troubled his soul. The sun sank in a copper blaze of glory. The Professor shook his head, and took a turn around the graveyard.

On his return to the Toshiba, he read his day's work so far, but it all looked a little boring, and he couldn't really make head or tail of it. Half heartedly, he drew his conclusions:

"9. ULTIMATE PERSPECTIVE
From an Absolutist perspective, all is One. The dream is a dream,
dreamed by the Absolute, and as 'I am That - my Self', it is my sole
dream. Only 'I' have the first hand experience of 'That'. This concept
can only be experienced when the latent, habitual, conditioned
tendencies are all expelled through ruthless Self-examination, and
the mind is surrendered to the truth I have to-day outlined."

***

Which is what? The learned Professor stopped typing with a jolt. Even if it feels true, he must never reveal his confession to the world; otherwise his whole delightful game of metaphysical disputation and assertion will cease and he will be bereft of his occupation, livelihood and sole raison d'etre.

Dr Wiseacre feels better now - he has relieved himself of extreme mental torment. He goes downstairs with a book by one of his colleagues in Tubingen, who argues those hard questions arising from Advanced Consciousness Studies: it is a sort of hobby.

"The Stoat is Totally Different, therefore the Weasel is Weaselly Right: Discuss." He'll set the students that question, and amuse himself with their responses, then demolish them with his nut cracker brain and acerbic wit – ah, such Socratic irony! His walk gave him an appetite. Ha, ha, ha, he chortled to himself. A Dream within a dream, you stupid dolt! Forget such an absurd fantasy even if it may be true.

Now for some of Mrs Felsenberg's thick frankfurter and lentil soup, which she serves on a Monday!

BOOKS

O is a symbol of the world, of oneness and unity. In different cultures it also means the "eye," symbolizing knowledge and insight. We aim to publish books that are accessible, constructive and that challenge accepted opinion, both that of academia and the "moral majority."

Our books are available in all good English language bookstores worldwide. If you don't see the book on the shelves ask the bookstore to order it for you, quoting the ISBN number and title. Alternatively you can order online (all major online retail sites carry our titles) or contact the distributor in the relevant country, listed on the copyright page.

See our website www.o-books.net for a full list of over 500 titles, growing by 100 a year.

And tune in to myspiritradio.com for our book review radio show, hosted by June-Elleni Laine, where you can listen to the authors discussing their books.